THE MAN I THOUGHT I TRUSTED

TWO-FACED #3

E. L. TODD

HARTWICK PUBLISHING

Hartwick Publishing

The Man I Thought I Trusted

Copyright © 2020 by E. L. Todd

All rights reserved.

No part of this book may be reproduced in any form or by any electronic or mechanical means, including information storage and retrieval systems, without written permission from the author, except for the use of brief quotations in a book review.

CONTENTS

1. Carson — 1
2. Carson — 13
3. Carson — 25
4. Dax — 37
5. Dax — 43
6. Dax — 51
7. Dax — 55
8. Dax — 63
9. Carson — 71
10. Carson — 89
11. Carson — 95
12. Charlie — 99
13. Dax — 109
14. Carson — 115
15. Dax — 123
16. Carson — 131
17. Dax — 137
18. Carson — 143
19. Dax — 161
20. Charlie — 173
21. Carson — 177
22. Dax — 187
23. Carson — 195
24. Carson — 209
25. Dax — 215
26. Carson — 227
27. Dax — 239
28. Carson — 243
29. Carson — 251
30. Dax — 253
31. Carson — 259

| 32. Dax | 261 |
| Epilogue | 267 |

1

CARSON

I woke up the next morning feeling the heat from the sunlight on my face. Last night, the window showed the thriving city outside, lights glimmering like beacons, but now it was a brilliant day and the lights from the buildings had dimmed. I arched my back and stretched my arms above my head, sighing as my body enjoyed the comfortable mattress and the high-end sheets that cuddled me all night long. I couldn't remember the last time I'd slept so well, woke up in the morning and felt like I could do anything. Was it just the bedding? Or was it the man beside me?

I opened my eyes and looked at Dax. He was on his back with his head slightly tilted my way, his eyes closed and his jaw relaxed. With every breath he took, his chest rose slightly, his flat stomach chiseled even when he was unconscious. The sheets were loose around his waist as if he got hot during the night and pushed them away, and a bit of his happy trail was visible far below. Veins covered his tanned skin on his muscular arms and the abs below his belly button. Awake or not awake, this man was beautiful.

Yeah, it definitely wasn't the bedding that made me sleep so long.

It was the man.

I shifted closer to him and pressed a kiss to his shoulder, my tongue taking a gentle swipe so I could taste him. Seeing his face first thing in the morning was more exhilarating than the view from his penthouse. His scruff was even thicker than it had been the night before, and I loved that masculine look.

My eyes glanced down to the sheets over his waist and noticed the distinct outline of his bulging cock.

Damn, I could get used to this.

I crawled over him and pulled back the sheets slightly so I could press a gentle kiss to the top of his dick.

He didn't wake up, but an almost inaudible moan emerged from his closed lips.

I got out of bed and helped myself to his discarded shirt on the floor. I got a better look at his bedroom, the seventy-inch TV mounted on the wall, the high-end furniture, the armchair outside his closet where he sat to put shoes on every morning.

His bedroom was almost as big as my apartment.

I left the bedroom and walked down the hallway, seeing a whole other hallway emerge at an intersection in the corridor. I had no idea where it led, and I wasn't nosy enough to find out. I kept going and headed to the main room where the kitchen was located.

Floor-to-ceiling windows took up the entire back wall, and it was an open room, with the dining table, kitchen, and living room all in the same area. It was perfect for entertaining, even though I wasn't sure how much he hosted events.

Just this space alone was bigger than a single floor in my apartment building. That must mean every unit took up an entire floor of the building.

How could one person need this much space?

I walked into the kitchen and looked for the coffeepot. Of course, he didn't have something basic. It was a big, shiny device that looked like it belonged on the counter of a coffee shop. It took some time to figure out how to work the stupid thing and make myself a cup of joe.

His wealth didn't intimidate me, and it didn't make me think higher of him either. It was just a part of who he was, and I'd have to get used to it. When he said I would've thought of him differently if I'd known he was a billionaire the night we met, he was right. I would've made unfair assumptions about who he was instead of seeing the man behind the wallet. I would have assumed he was arrogant, snobbish, egotistical... entitled. But he wasn't a jerk like the other rich people I had to deal with, so I actually was grateful he'd deceived me.

Otherwise, this might never have happened.

I wouldn't have found the man I was supposed to be with.

I took a seat at the dining table that was next to the window and drank my coffee as I looked at my emails on my phone.

A text message popped up from Charlie. *So...you never came home last night.*

I grinned. *Nope.*

Are you going to come home tonight?

Double nope.

Did you get that D?

Only all night...

Finally. Is Kat okay?

The mention of her immediately brought down my mood. *She's pretty down, honestly. But she'll come around.*

Charlie didn't text me back.

The sound of footfalls came to my ears as Dax entered the kitchen. Barefoot and just in his sweatpants, he stood at the coffeemaker and made himself a cup before he took a drink and joined me at the dining table. "Morning, sweetheart." He set his coffee mug on the table then leaned down to kiss me.

I tilted my head back and took his lips, exchanging a slow and seductive kiss that made me want to go straight back to the bedroom.

When he pulled away slightly, he gave me an affectionate look before he pulled out the chair and took a seat beside me. His eyes were heavy-lidded and sleepy, and his hair was messy from all the times I'd fisted it through the night. He gripped the mug by the handle and brought it to his lips for another drink.

I saw him sitting there shirtless with those broad shoulders and strong chest, and I knew I could stare at him like that every single day. The deep, emotional attachment was still there, but the physical lust had turned on as if a button had been pressed. I wanted this man—every chance I got.

He watched me stare at him, relaxing in the chair with slight affection in his gaze. "Did you tell Charlie?"

"He texted me a couple minutes ago. And yes, he was very happy that his best friend got laid."

He chuckled. "Good. He's gonna be happy pretty often, then."

My eyes glanced over his body, giving him a seductive stare that showed how much I wanted him. "Hell yeah..."

He gave a slight smile before he sipped his coffee again.

"I told him I wouldn't be home until tomorrow morning. If that's okay..." I wanted to be in Dax's arms every night. I never wanted to sleep in a bed alone when there was such a better alternative. Why be alone when I could have this perfect, gorgeous, wonderful man hold me through the night?

"You could move in, and I would say that's okay."

I chuckled before I grabbed my coffee and took a drink, not taking his words seriously.

But he just looked at me...like he was dead serious.

When he'd said those three little words last night, I hadn't expected to hear them. And I also hadn't expected my own reaction, to say them back, to hear the sincerity in my voice as well as feel it in my heart. It was natural, and for the first time, I didn't overthink my actions. I just lived in the moment —with him.

With his fingers wrapped around the handle of his mug, he stared at me, like he was thinking about the same moment.

I didn't have any regrets. It was the happiest I'd been in a really long time. Well, not *that* long, but it felt that way.

Now I was glad Evan had been in the bar that night just so Dax would kiss me. Who knew something so good could come out of that?

Steam rose from his cup, the black liquid frothy at the top from the way the beans were ground up in the machine. "What did you want to do today?"

"Oh, come on." I released an uncontrollable snort at the stupid question.

"What?" He drank from his coffee.

"Don't *what* me. You know exactly what I want to do. And I want to do it all day and all night…"

His eyes shifted away slightly, a handsome grin coming onto his lips like my desire was flattering to him. Women wanted to jump his bones all the time, but somehow my enthusiasm was special. "What about food?"

"Oh yeah." Shit, I hadn't thought of that, which was an important thing to consider, at least for me.

"I know my woman can't go very long without eating."

"Well, we can take a break for that. But that's it." I waved my index finger. "Nothing else."

He took another drink of his coffee before he rose to his feet. "How about we make some breakfast, then?"

My eyes absorbed his muscled frame, immediately picturing that handsome face between my thighs, his scruff scratching me and turning me on. But my pussy and my stomach were at war with each other, because a loud grumbling sound filled the dining room.

He grinned before he turned away. "There's my answer."

I FACED the back of the couch with my hands gripping the edge, my back arched, tears glistening in the corners of my eyes as my body was thrust forward every time he pushed inside me. His hand gripped the back of my neck aggressively, while his other hand held my hip, his body working hard to hit me deep over and over. "God...yes." My moans turned incoherent, and I started to scream as I came around his dick for the tenth time that weekend. "Fuck...yes." The tears escaped the corners of my eyes and fell down my cheeks.

He groaned as he listened to me come, his fingers digging into the back of my neck even deeper.

The sex was so much better than it used to be, good, sweaty, aggressive...so damn unbelievable. When I finished my high, I lowered my neck to rest my forehead on the back of the couch, catching my breath as my tightness released his dick.

He wrapped his arm across my chest and pulled me against him, his chest against my back. He rocked inside me deeply, holding me tight with his face pressed into my neck. He breathed and groaned, about to come inside me with a potent release.

"Fuck that pussy..."

He made a loud groan as he released, his big, fat dick throbbing inside me as it gave me his seed. We'd been fucking like rabbits in spring, and he still wasn't shooting blanks. White globs of arousal dripped from my entrance every single time.

He continued to thrust until he was completely finished. Then his arms squeezed me tightly as he panted into my ear, his sweaty chest rubbing against my soaked skin. He started to soften when he was finished, like his body couldn't go anymore after the fuck-a-thon we'd had all weekend. His batteries were officially drained.

I loved making love to this man, but I loved the bomb-as-fuck sex too. God, it was so good. This man was *so* good.

He pulled out of me then stepped into the bathroom to clean up. He returned with a handful of tissues.

I took them to clean myself up. "What a gentleman."

He grinned before he pulled on his sweatpants again and walked into the kitchen to make dinner.

I put on my underwear and his shirt before I joined him.

He opened the fridge and grabbed a couple things before leaving them on the counter.

I lifted myself onto the granite countertop so my legs could dangle over the edge. I leaned back against the cabinet, my eyes tired and heavy after all the good chemicals dumped into my blood. All this hot sex made me so happy and relaxed. My coochie had never been so satisfied. I watched him move around the kitchen, still wanting more...believe it or not.

How could I not? Look at that hunk of man.

He started to cook on the stove, letting everything sizzle in the oiled-up pans before he turned to look at me. "Really? Again?"

"Yep." I was completely unapologetic about it.

He grabbed a spatula and stirred everything before he came close to me and stood in front of me.

My legs immediately circled his waist, and my ankles locked together. "Now, you can't go anywhere."

He brought his face close to mine and stared at my lips for a long time. "Like I'd want to." He leaned in and pressed a kiss to the corner of my mouth.

My hands touched his hard chest as we listened to our dinner sizzle in the hot pans. "I didn't think the sex could get any better."

His confident gaze was locked on to my face. "It's always better when you're in love."

My eyes softened as I continued to feel his muscular chest, my legs pulling him in just a little bit closer.

His hands flattened on the granite on either side of me, and he brought himself even closer, his forehead resting on mine, our dinner abandoned. "You're so beautiful when you let me in like this."

I felt like a completely different woman now that I'd given him full access to my heart. Carefree, trusting, and deliriously happy, I gave him everything I had.

And it was so easy to do.

He pressed his face into my neck and gave me a few kisses before he pulled away and returned to making our food.

My knees came together automatically with his absence, and I pulled them to my chest as I watched him cook, his tight, muscular back glistening with sweat. "What made you decide to live in such a big place?"

He flipped the meat and added more oil to the veggies. "It wasn't the size that attracted me. Rather, the building, the location, and the security. The other residents guard their privacy and keep to themselves, which is perfect for me because I'm the same way."

"I guess that makes sense."

He stood over the stove, sexy and shirtless, his body tight and chiseled whether he was tense or relaxed. He was so fit that he always looked strong.

"How long have you been here?"

"About seven years now."

"Oh..."

He turned back to me, silently asking for an explanation for my less-than-positive remark.

"Does that mean you lived here with your ex-wife?"

He nodded. "It was one of the few things I got to keep in the divorce."

For a split second, it made me feel weird to be in the same penthouse where she used to live, in the bedroom where she used to sleep, at the dining table where she used to eat, but then I realized it was a long time ago and it shouldn't matter. She didn't deserve him in the first place.

When the food was done, he plated everything then

handed my dinner to me. He leaned against the opposite counter, facing me, and ate where he stood, holding the plate with one hand with his fork in the other.

"Ten thousand square feet in this place and you want to eat like this?" I teased.

He sliced his fork into his tender chicken and shrugged before he placed a bite in his mouth. "You look too cute to move."

I liked that answer. "This is really good." I took a few bites, my feet still dangling over the edge.

"Do I cook better than Charlie?"

I squirmed on the spot. "No comment..."

"Oh, come on. You can tell me."

"You're putting me in a really awkward position. If I say your cooking is better and he finds out about it...he'll never cook for me again, which means I'll starve. If I say he's better, I might not get that bomb-as-fuck sex anymore."

"Bomb as fuck?" he asked, his eyes down on his food.

"Yes, that's the best description I can think of."

"I'll take that as a compliment." He grabbed a stalk of asparagus and took a bite of the first half, looking at me as he did it. "Can I ask you something personal?"

"Anything."

He did a double take when he heard what I said, his chin rising slightly so he could focus on me once more. Then a gentle smile came over that handsome face. "I'm not asking from a place of jealousy. I'm just curious—"

"No."

"No, what? You didn't give me a chance to finish."

"Nothing has ever happened with Charlie. Ever." My lovers always asked me this question because they couldn't understand our friendship. Dax had already asked me this before, but he must have wanted to ask again now that I was more vulnerable than I used to be.

He looked amused by my response. "You get that question a lot, then?"

I nodded. "And my answer has never changed. Why do you ask?"

He shrugged. "You guys just have a really deep connection. When we're playing basketball together, you can communicate telepathically. I've never seen anything like it."

I continued to eat. "You've never had a girl friend?"

He shook his head. "None that I haven't slept with. I guess my only female friend would be my sister, but that doesn't really count." He finished his food quickly and left his plate on the counter beside him.

"Well, it happens. There's never been *any* attraction between us. Even if there were, I would never jeopardize our relationship for anything."

He crossed arms over his chest as he watched me. "I guess I find it hard to believe because it's impossible not to be attracted to you, not to think you're special, not to think you're a bomb-as-fuck woman. How is it Charlie doesn't see that? I have no idea."

I looked down at my food because I didn't know what to say. It was such a compliment, a really nice one coming from a man like him. "You know, a lot of men I meet think I'm a bitch. I'm ambitious, opinionated, independent—those aren't exactly sexy traits to most people. You're one of the few men who actually sees value in them. So, it's not me—it's you." He was a perfect man for me, someone who admired my spunk and was man enough to handle it. "Charlie doesn't like that kind of woman. Look at Denise. She's very quiet, submissive. And that's fine, there's nothing wrong with that, but I'm just not Charlie's type."

He stared at me for a long time with that absorbing gaze, pondering everything I said. Then he gave a slight nod. "I guess I can understand that."

"Not everyone thinks I'm as special as you do."

"Well, that worked out in my favor." He gave a slight smile. "I'm man enough for you, and I know most men are boys, so that's not surprising." He grabbed his plate and carried it to the sink so he could rinse it off and leave it for his housekeeper.

It was nice to be in a relationship with someone who admired me so openly, who was excited for my accomplishments, who could handle my fire with his own inferno. I suddenly felt a jolt of fear, because I realized I had something really amazing...and I wouldn't know what to do if I ever lost it.

When I walked in the door to my apartment on Monday morning, Charlie was sitting at the dining table with a cup of coffee next to his laptop. After he sipped his coffee, he raised his eyes and looked at me for a few seconds. "Wow, you look totally different."

I hadn't worn makeup in several days because I didn't bring any in my overnight bag, and I was wearing the exact outfit I'd been wearing on Friday night. It was the ultimate walk of shame. I threw my purse on the table and kicked off my heels. "That's what a fuck-a-thon does to you."

He chuckled. "Way to rub it in, man."

I made myself a cup of coffee and sat across from him. "It'll happen for you, Charlie."

He didn't look at his computer. Instead, he just stared at me. "It's nice to see you happy." The statement came out of nowhere, containing a noticeable level of affection that showed his sincerity.

I gave a smile. "Thanks..."

"Now I need you to move in with him or marry him so you'll get out of my hair." He turned back to his work and looked at his computer.

"Like you could afford this place without me."

His eyes were back on me instantly. "I probably could if you didn't eat half my lunch every day. That shit adds up."

I rolled my eyes and took a drink from my mug. "I pay for all the groceries, alright? And I throw in free condoms too. You basically got your own Instacart worker over here." I snapped my fingers and pointed at myself.

He chuckled. "Fuck, I *hate* condoms. I want to be in a real relationship again so I don't have to wear them anymore..." He gave me a serious look, like he expected me to do something about that.

It was too early in the morning to talk about Kat. "Yeah, it is pretty great." It was so sexy not to be separated by latex, to feel each other so intimately, to feel his seed every time he gave it to me.

He gave an irritated sigh. "Jealous."

I smiled and brought my mug to my lips. "You should be."

2

CARSON

"So, you've been doing the nasty-nasty, then?" Matt asked from across the booth in the bar, his beer sitting in front of him.

"Might be..." I gave a shrug before I took a sip of my wine.

Charlie drank from his glass and scanned the bar as if he expected Denise to appear out of nowhere.

"Come on," Matt said. "You tell us more details than we want to know about *everything,* and now all of a sudden, you're closed like a clam?"

"Why do you want to know?" I countered.

"Because he's hot." Matt raised his arms like he couldn't believe I didn't understand his interest. "I want the 4-1-1. So, size, skill level, all that good stuff." He snapped his fingers a couple times. "Chop-chop."

I tried to suppress a grin because I couldn't believe I was the only one who got to know those details. Women had come before me, but I suspected it wasn't as good for them as it was for me. I knew how Dax felt about me, so when we were together, it was special. "What about Jeremy?"

"Yeah," Charlie said. "Do you think he'd appreciate you wanting the details of some other hot guy?"

"Are you kidding me?" Matt said. "He thinks Dax's hot too. He's always thought he was hot. He's gotten to see him in the locker room a few times, but I haven't had the pleasure."

I swirled my glass of wine before I set it down. "He's very good in bed. I'll tell you that much." I gave a thumbs-up.

"Obviously," Matt said, rolling his eyes. "I already knew that."

Charlie glanced at the entryway before he nudged Matt in the side. "Look, your boyfriend's here."

"No." I pointed my index finger at my chest. "*My* boyfriend is here. Your boyfriend is at work or the gym or something." I turned to Dax and raised my hand in the air so he could easily find us.

Affection entered his gaze when he spotted me, and he walked over in jeans and a shirt, looking sexy with those broad shoulders and that chiseled waist and narrow hips.

He slid into the booth beside me, his arm wrapping around my shoulders as he leaned in and kissed me. "Hey, sweetheart."

I grabbed the front of his shirt and pulled him in deeper, giving him a hard kiss like I hadn't seen him in months. I didn't care about the guys sitting across from us, and I kissed him longer than I should for being in a public place.

Did I give a damn? Nope.

But he was totally into it, smiling as he kissed me, like he loved all the attention.

When I pulled away, I looked back at the guys. Matt stared with wide eyes like he enjoyed the front-row show.

Charlie kept drinking his beer and looking across the bar as if he hadn't noticed anything.

"What were you guys talking about?" Dax pulled his arm from my shoulders and rested his hand on my thigh. His long fingers gave my leg a possessive and masculine squeeze, making me feel like I was still all his even when the kissing stopped.

I gave a blunt answer. "Our bomb-as-fuck sex."

A slight smile moved onto his lips, like he was a little embarrassed but also flattered that I was praising him to my friends. "I hope I came off well."

"Definitely," Matt blurted.

"It certainly made Charlie jealous." I looked at my best friend, who was still staring across the bar.

He let out a deep sigh before he drank from his beer. "Hopefully, I won't have to be jealous much longer..."

"What's going to happen with that?" Matt had stopped obsessing over Dax and his excellent bedroom skills and shifted to a different subject, one I'd rather avoid. "So, she's even seen their mutual attraction with her own eyes. Does that mean she accepts it?"

Charlie finally turned his gaze back to us, participating in the conversation once again.

Dax waved down the waitress and ordered himself a scotch, his hand on my thigh the entire time, making it clear to anyone who watched that he was off the market for good.

I gave an exaggerated shrug. "Dude, I don't know..." This drama had nothing to do with me, but somehow, I was in the center of it. It was exhausting, borderline childish, because I felt like I was in high school again. "Bottom line, this is always going to be hard for her, and I don't know what to do about it. There's no clear answer, you know?"

Charlie didn't have much of a reaction, but he released a long and quiet sigh, his eyes dropping with his mood. "I don't mean to sound like an ass, but she needs to get over it."

I took a drink of my wine before I looked at him. "I agree, but that was an asshole way of putting it."

"Don't you think she should know the truth?" Matt turned to look at Charlie. "Remember the first time you told me how you felt about Denise? You said you felt like shit, but there was nothing you could do to stop it. It was mushy-mushy bullshit, and that's saying something coming from a gay man."

Charlie gave me a hard look.

Matt turned back to me. "Maybe we should just tell her. She would understand the significance of the situation and know this is really important to Charlie. And if she ever loved him, she would want him to be happy."

I knew it was more complicated than that because her heart was on the line. "How would you feel if the person you were in love with left you because they found love with somebody else? That was the mysterious reason your relationship ended? Yes, I think it would be exactly what she needs to hear to move on, but think of the cost. Think of the way it will make her feel. It's...cruel."

Dax started to rub my thigh through my jeans, silently comforting me because he knew this was hard to endure. I didn't want my best friend to be crushed, and I didn't want my other best friend to be miserable.

Matt gave a shrug. "I guess I'm biased because Charlie is my best friend and I want him to have whatever he wants. I care about Kat too, obviously, but...I don't know." He rubbed the back of his neck, his mood turning sour like Charlie's.

Charlie rested his hand on top of his glass and looked down at the golden liquid inside. "I did everything I could to protect her from getting hurt, kept as much integrity as I could through the process because I did love her, and a part of me always will, but I can't make any more sacrifices for my happiness. I waited long enough to pursue what I really want. I can't put any more time on hold for somebody else. Maybe that makes me sound like a jerk, but I don't care anymore."

I was literally in the middle of this whole ordeal, the nucleus that pulled everything close together. I could just step aside and let Charlie figure it out, but I suspected it would break hearts on the way. I wanted my hands to remain clean, but not if it caused more pain.

He spoke again. "How would you feel if this were you and

Dax? That the only man you really want is off-limits because Kat used to date him?"

If I couldn't have Dax, it would be unbearable. Now that I'd allowed myself to really feel again, I'd realized how deeply I'd fallen for him.

Charlie stared at me, silently telling me exactly what he wanted me to do.

I dropped my gaze down to my glass and stared at the red wine that warmed my stomach as I sipped it. "Fine..."

Dax turned to me, slightly confused by my statement.

Charlie angled his body away. "Thank you."

"What just happened?" Dax asked, his eyes moving back and forth between Charlie and me.

Matt answered. "They just did one of the weird telepathic things they do." He pointed at his eyes then pointed between us. "You know, talking without actually talking."

Charlie directed his gaze to Dax. "She's going to tell Kat the truth."

I released a quiet sigh. "And I'm not looking forward to it at all."

We watched the game in the living room, enjoying slices of pizza and beer.

Dax had already become one of the guys, fitting into our group so perfectly, even if we weren't seeing each other.

"You can't be serious." Dax sat forward with his arms on his knees, looking at Charlie in the armchair. "He's not the best quarterback in football history. A couple Super Bowl rings don't mean a whole lot in the grand scheme of things."

Charlie fired back. "But there're a lot of teams that have never won a Super Bowl ring, and that means a lot." He pointed at Dax with the neck of his bottle before he turned back to the television.

Jeremy and Matt sat together on the other couch, cuddled close as they drank their beers and relaxed.

Dax shook his head. "I don't agree. I think there're a lot of other quarterbacks who have more talent."

"The guy is pushing forty," Charlie countered. "Most guys retire in their early thirties, if not before."

Dax continued to disagree. "Not quarterbacks. I still think the guy's overrated." He turned back to the game and watched the TV.

I sat beside him, and with my hand across his thigh, I gave him a gentle squeeze that told him I didn't care to listen to him argue about football with my best friend.

That immediately got his attention.

He turned back to me, showing a special look in his eyes that he only gave to me, like I was the morning light at dawn. "I'm not paying enough attention to you, am I?"

I shook my head and squeezed him a little tighter as my fingers glided closer to his crotch.

His eyes darkened before he leaned in and kissed me, a slow and seductive kiss like nobody was there to witness it. When he pulled away, he rubbed his nose against mine. "Is that better?"

I nodded. "A bit."

There was a knock on the door before it opened. Denise stepped inside, wearing black leggings with high brown boots and a loose white sweater.

Charlie was about to take a drink of his beer, but he stilled just so he could stare at her. He looked like he wanted to shove his fist into his mouth—and bite down hard just to control himself.

It was impossible that she wasn't aware of Charlie's obsession, but she continued to act like she had no idea. "Hey, guys. Any pizza left?"

Charlie seemed too spellbound by her appearance to say

anything, so I did the talking. "Just a few slices. Beers in the fridge."

She walked to the fridge and opened it.

Charlie turned around completely in his chair so he could stare at her, doing a full 180.

I snapped my fingers at his face and mouthed, "Dude, get it together."

He mouthed back, "Oh, you're one to talk."

I continued the exchange in silence. "Oh, shut up."

He flipped me the bird.

Dax's gaze shifted back and forth between us like he had no idea what we were saying.

Denise came into the living room with her open beer in hand. "Where should I sit? I've got a couple on each couch."

"Don't sit there." Charlie pointed at the couch where Dax and I sat. "Not unless you want a live sex show."

I rolled my eyes. "What an exaggeration..."

She turned to Matt and Jeremy next. "What about them?"

"Not much better," Matt said. "You're probably better off sitting in that armchair together."

I knew *exactly* what he was doing.

Denise turned to him. "Do you mind?"

Does he mind? Ha.

Like a deer in the headlights, Charlie just stared at her as if he couldn't believe what she'd just asked. He gathered his bearings and shifted his body to the side. "Not at all."

She took the seat beside him, part of her body slightly on top of his, and she drank her beer as she looked at the TV.

Charlie pressed his body against the other side of the armchair as much as possible, like he was doing everything he could to not touch her—even though all he wanted to do was touch her.

Matt looked at Charlie and gave an exaggerated wink.

That made me flip Matt the bird.

Denise drank her beer then turned to ask Charlie a question about the game. "I don't follow sports. What's going on here?"

Charlie answered her question, and the longer they talked together, the more he let down his guard. He stopped trying to stay away from her and let their two bodies naturally press together.

Dax wrapped his arm around my shoulders and turned his intention on me. He ignored the game as if he no longer cared about it the way he had just a few minutes ago. "Do you have plans next Saturday?"

"I better." I gave his thigh a possessive squeeze.

He gave that handsome smile I adored, like he lived for my enthusiasm, couldn't get enough of it. "I thought you could meet some of my friends."

"I have met your friends." I played basketball with them every Wednesday, got hot wings and pizza afterward.

Jeremy ran his fingers through Matt's short hair. "He means his rich, asshole friends..."

Dax didn't refute the claim. "Yes...*those* friends."

"Will I like them?" I asked.

He shrugged. "Not sure. But you'll definitely be able to handle them. After the mob, these guys will be a piece of cake." He looked at me affectionately, like my wild side was somehow endearing.

"Well, I actually like the mob. If you put aside all the stealing and murder, they're pretty cool guys."

He chuckled and brought me in close so he could press a kiss to my neck.

"What are we doing?" I asked, still feeling the tingle on my skin after his lips were gone.

"I have this charity dinner on Saturday night."

"Oh. So, this is like an *event*."

He shrugged. "I guess. But they'll be there, so I thought it was a good time to introduce you."

"Sounds kind of stuffy."

He shrugged in affirmation.

"Is there an alleyway nearby…?"

He smiled again before his lips moved back to my neck, giving me a longer embrace. "I'm sure there is. And if not, I'll definitely find one."

Denise and the guys left, so we picked up the empty beer bottles and pizza boxes and tossed them.

Dax stood with his hands in his pockets and moved toward the door, like he expected to leave.

I threw the last few bottles away without looking at him. "What do you think you're doing?"

He stopped in front of the door, not wearing a smile on his lips but definite playfulness in his eyes. "Do you want me to stay?"

"No." I tied the strings to the top of the bag, and I set it on the floor near the kitchen island so Charlie could throw it out. "I'm telling you."

And just like that, he looked completely enamored of me once again. He came closer and grabbed the bag from the floor. "I'll take care of this."

"You don't have to do that."

He nodded behind me to where Charlie stood. "I think I'm getting better at this telepathy thing because I'm pretty sure he wants to talk to you." He grabbed the other bag too and carried it into the hallway.

When I turned around to look at Charlie, I stopped in place because he looked furious. His normally smiling mouth was clenched tight like he was suppressing a scream, and his large hands gripped the edge of the counter like he might break it off into pieces. "Wow, what happened?"

"What happened? Did you see Denise sitting in my lap? I'm surprised my dick didn't hurt her back."

I rolled my eyes at his flattering assessment of himself. "Okay now…"

"You said you would talk to Kat, so talk to her. What the hell are you waiting for? It's not like I can just go out and pick up a girl at this point. I have a celibate relationship with Denise, and it fucking sucks."

"I will talk to her. It's been a busy week—" Busy fucking Dax.

"Yes, I've noticed. I have to sit there and listen to you talk about all the good sex you're getting, while I'm sitting with Denise and trying to stay soft. You're the biggest cockblock in the world."

"How dare you! I am not a cockblock."

"Then talk to Kat and get it over with. I know you. I know you're procrastinating."

"I'm not a procrastinator. I get my articles done early—not just on time."

"You procrastinate for shit you don't want to do. Remember when it was your turn to clean the apartment, and you dragged your feet for three months?"

I crossed my arms over my chest and rolled my eyes. "So not the same thing."

"I have to listen to you and Dax go at it tonight while I'm sleeping alone. I'm happy for you, I really am, but I want to be happy too. Come on, think about it. The four of us could go out together all the time. How awesome would it be if Denise and I ended up together? I would be your brother-in-law."

Yes, that did sound like a dream come true. Charlie was already my brother, already my family, and I was actually closer to him than my own sister. It might bring Denise and me closer together. "You're only focusing on the good, not the bad. If I don't handle this right, we might lose Kat as a friend. Do you want that?"

His eyes became clouded with irritation. "Of course I

don't. But Jesus Christ, it's time to move on. Get it done within three days, or I'll tell her myself."

It would be way worse coming from him than me. At least with me, she could cry and not be embarrassed about it. At least she could show her full heart without having to contain it. "I'll talk to her tomorrow."

"Yeah, you said that last time." He turned back to the kitchen and finished cleaning, giving me the cold shoulder.

Dax came back inside and walked to the sink. "You guys hash it out?" He washed his hands and patted them dry before he turned around to look at us.

"You could say that." Charlie grabbed his phone and headed to the hallway. "I told Carson to grow some balls." He was gone from our sight, and his bedroom door shut a moment later.

After Dax watched him walk away, he turned back to me. "Kat?"

I nodded.

"I understand. If I couldn't be with you, I'd be losing my mind too." He left the kitchen and moved closer to me, his arms circling my waist and bringing me in close. "Ready for bed?"

"Yes. And I'm not ready to go to sleep..."

"Me neither."

We went to my bedroom and shut the door behind us. I liked to go to sleep the second we were done with sex, so I did my nighttime routine before, like washing off my makeup and brushing my teeth. I know I didn't look as good, but he didn't seem to care. He seemed to want me just the same.

When I came back to bed, I took off my clothes and my panties and crawled into bed beside him, the sheets covering his waist but all his chiseled masculinity visible in the dark bedroom.

Once my back was to the mattress, he was on top of me, between my legs, his weight pressing me into the sheets.

My hands dug into his hair and cradled his face close to mine. "I was going to be on top."

"You can be on top next time." He positioned himself and entered, stretching me wide and making me moan. When he was balls deep, he released a masculine sigh, like it was so good to feel me like this. He paused for a moment as he looked at me, our bodies together, our souls wrapped into one.

My arms and legs wrapped around him, and I breathed against his mouth, loving how wonderful it felt to have this man so close to my heart. We hadn't said those special words to each other since the first time, but I liked it that way. I liked knowing how he felt about me in the silent moments, when he went out of his way to do something for me and I didn't have to ask, when he looked at me like I was the most special thing in the world. I knew how he felt without his having to say it, and that was better than the actual words.

And he knew how I felt about him, because it was obvious in everything that I did.

3

CARSON

My phone rang on my desk in my cubicle at work.

I answered while keeping my eyes focused on the last words I was writing on my laptop. "Boss bitch."

Vince chuckled. "I want to talk to you in my office."

"Be there in a sec." I hung up and spun around in my chair before I got to my feet and walked to the other side of the room.

Charlie intercepted me on the way. "Got plans tonight?" He turned around in his chair so he could face me, wearing a brown jacket with a black shirt underneath.

"Not with you."

"Not with Dax either, right?"

"Well, I *always* have plans with him. He's just my last appointment of the night." I waggled my eyebrows.

He couldn't suppress the smile my words caused.

"I'm going to Kat's later. Don't expect a happy ending."

"I'm not. I just want some progress." He turned around in his chair again and went back to his laptop.

I walked across the floor and entered my boss's office. "Boss bitch is here. What can I do for you?"

Vince was a laid-back guy who knew how to take a joke.

As long as you did your work right and submitted it on time, he couldn't care less about your professional decorum. He was a great boss. "I've got something for you. I know you're already juggling a couple things, but I thought this would be a good fit." He set a folder at the edge of his desk, and that motherfucker was *thick*. It was stuffed with pages and pages.

"As long as it's not the Lifestyle section, I'm good." No offense to anyone who was interested in gardening tips, but I didn't care about stuff like that. I grabbed the folder and took a seat so I could open it and take a look. "The pharmaceutical business." I nodded slightly. "They're more corrupt than the mob."

"Definitely. They're cutting opioids with dangerous levels of fentanyl, which is causing more people to either overdose or get sick, and then they end up in the hospital. Not only that, but the cost of insulin just increased by three hundred percent. And you know who benefited from that?"

"Oh, I know exactly who. The CEO." These criminals were amateurs, thinking they could continue shady money moves and nobody would notice. In this day and age, people noticed *everything*. With the internet, there was no way to be secretive about anything anymore.

He gave me a look of approval. "Bring them down, boss bitch."

"Oh, I will." I stood up and flipped my hair before I strutted out of his office. "There's definitely going to be some death threats."

"But they won't be able to shake you down."

I turned around when I reached his door. "No, honey. *I'll* be the one making the death threats."

Kat and I sat in her apartment and ate the burritos I'd picked up on the way from the office. We sat at the dining table and had a couple of beers since our usual choice of wine wouldn't pair with our Mexican food.

She seemed to be in mostly good spirits, but there was definitely a sadness to her eyes that never went away, even when she laughed. "I'm really glad you and Dax worked it out. I know what he did was shady, but I get it. I have a lot of rich clients who are super paranoid and private. They don't want anyone to know they're rich, and they only socialize with other rich people because they know they won't care that they're loaded."

It was water under the bridge at this point. I forgave him and moved on. He and I were from different worlds, but when we were together, that didn't really matter. "It's fine. I've let it go. I know he's more than that."

"Good. So, now that you're officially dating a billionaire, what's it like?"

I shrugged. "Not any different from dating a regular guy. It's not like he talks about how much money he has all the time. And I told him I don't like fancy places, so we get sandwiches and stuff. Honestly, it doesn't feel any different."

"Doesn't he have yachts and second and third homes?"

"I don't know. I've never asked."

She chuckled. "I bet he's so glad he found you. I think ninety-five percent of women would be obsessed with his wealth, and you seem to forget about it."

"All I care about is the man underneath the suit. So, yes, I think I do forget about it." He didn't need the money to compensate for any shortcomings. He would be the perfect man even if he were broke.

I knew Kat was in a tough place in life right now, and it meant a lot to me that she was still happy for me. That was the kind of person she was, somebody who thought about others instead of herself. That was why this was so much harder. "So, how have you been doing since…you know?" Since Charlie acted like a cartoon with his tongue hanging out and drooling over Denise as she walked by.

Her mood immediately dropped as if a bulldozer had knocked her over. "I mean...it's been hard. I'm better now than I was that night, but it was still scarring to see the way Charlie was so hung up on her. I remember when he used to look at me like that..." Her eyes faded away, like she was living in the past, thinking of a cherished memory when they were happy together. She eventually came back to me. "But I guess I have to let that go." She swallowed the lump in her throat, and her eyes watered slightly. "But it'll pass. He'll find somebody else, and then that'll be it."

At the beginning of her statement, I had high hopes for this conversation, but then it took a nose dive. "What do you mean?"

"Charlie will meet somebody else and forget about Denise. The man is gorgeous, and I'm sure he's been with so many women since we broke up."

I had to handle this delicately, so I tried to choose my words carefully. "Kat, I'm having a hard time understanding why you're okay with him seeing other women...just not Denise. Do you have a problem with her?"

"No, not at all." She shook her head. "Just that I actually know her. But with these other women, I can always tell myself they aren't as good as me, stuff like that to make me feel better. But with Denise, I know exactly who she is, and that just makes it weird, you know? Your sister is great and everything, but I don't see much of a difference between us. So if he wants to be with her, why not with me? It's just uncomfortable. I thought Denise was a friend, so how could you be happy for your friend when they're seeing the man you thought would be your husband?" She released a sigh as she shook her head. "This isn't just some old boyfriend. He's the love of my life."

I could understand that last part easily. I talked about my

relationship with Dax openly to everybody, and everyone else did the same when they were seeing somebody. It would be hard to hear Denise talk openly about how happy she was with the man Kat wanted first. But Denise would never do something so cruel.

"He'll find somebody else. It'll burn out." She grabbed the burrito again and took a bite, but then she stared down at the inside of it like she wasn't even hungry, she just wanted something to do to make her feel better.

The silence continued for a long time.

And I let it.

My heart palpitations were starting to make me sick. I didn't get scared for any reason; I looked death in the face and didn't blink, but this was terrifying. I was about to deliver the harshest news ever. "Kat..."

She looked up from the burrito and stared at me.

I almost chickened out. The trust in her eyes made me feel like shit, because the one person she felt the most comfortable with was about to shatter her entire world. But it was better to come from me than Charlie. "I don't want to be the one to tell you this, but I think it would be better coming from me and not Charlie."

Her hand lost its grip on her burrito, and it slipped onto the paper plate, bits of rice getting everywhere.

Fuck, where did I start?

"What are you talking about?" she whispered.

"I know you don't want Charlie and Denise to be together, for valid reasons. But I think you need to understand that it's not just some fleeting attraction between two people. It's deeper than that."

"Oh my god...they are already seeing each other. They've been seeing each other this whole time—"

"No," I said quickly. "Nothing has happened between them. They've just been friends. But Charlie feels really strongly toward her, and while he doesn't want to hurt you, this is what he really wants. This is what he's always wanted..."

The look of death settled on her face, making her skin pale as milk, her lips white like she'd been drained of blood. "What are you trying to tell me, Carson?"

"He's felt this way about her for a really long time..."

She started to breathe hard and then even harder. "How long?"

I didn't answer her because I didn't need to.

She knew.

"Oh my god..." Her palm rubbed against her chest, and she dropped her chin as she braced herself for the blow. She closed her eyes when she knew the painful truth, when it hit her like a bus. "That was why he broke up with me..." Her eyes filled with tears, and she cupped her mouth to silence her sobs and her shock.

I felt so fucking sick.

She worked through so many microemotions—pain, anger, even briefly...calm. It was a lot to process in one sitting, and she continued to rub her chest as she tried to calm herself down. Then she looked at me again as if she'd had an epiphany. "You knew..."

I could just lie and say I didn't know until recently, but I didn't like to lie; that wasn't who I was. "You have to understand that I'm in the middle of this because I'm friends with both of you. This is why I didn't want you guys to go out in the first place—"

"I can't believe you knew this *entire* time and you didn't tell me. You made me look like a fucking idiot! I'm sitting here telling you I'm still in love with him and I hope we get back together, and you knew he dumped me for Denise while I went on and on... What the fuck, Carson?" She dragged her hands down her face, trembling. "I didn't even have the opportunity to keep some self-respect. You think I would have pouted over him and whined to you like that if I'd known the truth?"

This was why I didn't want to do this. "Everything you told me, I never shared with him. And everything he told me, I didn't share with you. I tried to stay as neutral as possible, so please don't be so angry with me. Don't focus on me, just on the message I provided to you. Charlie was the one who made that decision, he's the one who hurt you, not me. He was going to tell you himself, but we both agreed it would be better to come from me. I knew it would hurt less." I truly had good intentions, truly looked out for her more than she realized.

"It would hurt less that both the love of my life and my best friend lied to my face?"

I dropped my chin and stared at the table. "It wasn't like that. I promise you. We both really care about you and wanted to handle this the right way."

She shoved herself away from the table and got to her feet. "I feel so fucking stupid right now…"

"Kat—"

"Don't fucking *Kat* me. You don't deserve to call me that. The man I loved was in love with somebody else, and you didn't even have my back."

"He didn't tell me until after he ended things with you. I kept pestering him for the real reason because we both knew he was hiding something, and then he finally told me…and I couldn't believe it. He asked me not to tell you, so I couldn't. And I also thought it would be cruel if I did."

She was too emotional right now to see my side of things. "I was waiting around for *months,* hoping he would come back, and you knew the entire time he wouldn't." She threw her arms down. "What the fuck, Carson? What kind of friend are you?"

"What was I supposed to do?" I yelled back. "I'm friends with both of you, and that's made me a part of your relationship when I shouldn't be in that position."

"No." She faced off with me, her eyes wide-open and livid. "Your loyalties lie with him. I get it. You live with him, you work with him, he's your best friend. Well, he's your *real* best friend. You made me look like a fucking dumbass. That's fine. But fucking own up to it. I wasted so much time that could've been prevented if you'd had my back. But you didn't."

My worst nightmare was unfolding right in front of my eyes. I was about to lose my best friend—and it wasn't even my fault. "It wasn't like that—"

"Get out of my apartment, Carson. And tell Charlie I wish him and Denise the best." Her eyes watered with angry tears until they dripped down her cheeks to her lips. "Let yourself out."

When I approached the door to my apartment, I got a text from Dax. *How'd it go with Kat?*

I quickly fired a message back. *It was a nightmare.*

I'm sorry, sweetheart. Want to come over?

I just want to be alone. I slipped my phone into my pocket and stepped into the apartment.

Charlie stood up so fast he almost toppled over. "What happened?"

I set my laptop bag on the table and walked to the fridge because I needed a beer or glass of wine...just something with a decent alcohol content. "Read the room, Charlie." I settled on a beer and twisted off the cap to take a drink.

He was in his sweats and a t-shirt, like he had no plans for the night except to sit in front of the TV and wait for the sound of my keys in the door. "That bad?"

I set my beer on the counter. "She thinks I'm a shitty friend for not telling her."

"But you didn't know until after I broke it off."

"But I've known for ten months, Charlie. Every time she

mentioned you, I kept my mouth shut. I knew this would happen." I wanted to be mad at Charlie, but I couldn't. I couldn't even be mad at myself because there was no good way to handle this. No matter what decision I made, I was screwed. It was the situation, not me. "It's fucking shitty…but whatever." I drank my beer again.

Charlie studied me for a long time, visibly sympathetic and looking guilty. He bowed his head to the floor and dragged his hands down his face as he released a deep sigh. "Carson, I'm so sorry. I feel like shit for the way this has affected you. I want to say I should've listened to your advice and never gotten together with her, but that would be insulting to the relationship we had."

I grabbed my beer again and took another drink, just wanting to go to sleep and wake up tomorrow to a new day, a fresh start. "For the record, if you and Denise don't work out and it becomes really tense, I have to choose my sister. I want to say I would remain neutral and close with both of you, but I just learned how impossible that is." I knew I was just angry and bitter right now, so I should probably go to bed and shut up.

Charlie didn't respond to that, like he knew I didn't mean it and let it slide. "You just dropped the news on her. After you give her some time, I'm sure she'll come around. She's always been a pragmatic person."

"And you don't realize the one thing she's not pragmatic about is you." I stared at the beer in my hand, feeling the dread in my heart. Did I just lose a friend? Was there nothing I could do about it? It was so painful, like losing my parents all over again.

Charlie had no idea what to say to that. He stood there with his arms crossed over his chest, watching me as he breathed.

"I guess you can go for Denise now. No use waiting around at this point."

He still wore that somber look, like going after the woman he wanted was the last thing on his mind. "I really want things to be okay with Kat first—and clearly, they aren't."

"You want to know the worst part?" I set the beer on the counter and looked at him again. "She's not even mad at you. She's just mad at me. Only me. While I played Switzerland, she was pouring out her feelings to me. All the while, I knew you couldn't feel more differently toward her." I shook my head as I replayed her words in my mind. When she put it like that, I really did feel like a bitch. "Who listens to somebody say how much they love a guy and hope they can work it out, knowing the guy is head over heels for somebody else?"

"Don't do that." His voice came out quiet. "You're taking all the blame on yourself, and that's not fair. I'm your best friend, coworker, and roommate. Kat is your best friend, and to top it off, Denise is your sister. What the hell are you supposed to do?"

I raised my hands in the air in an exaggerated shrug. "No fucking idea. Maybe it's not me at all. Maybe it's just the situation. Still shitty, nonetheless. Kat and I will never get over this, and I can already tell she's going to pull away from all of us, and we'll stop seeing her altogether. When I run into her at the coffee shop, she'll duck out and act like she didn't see me. Time will pass, and it'll be hard to remember what it was like when we were friends at all." The emotional, poetic side of me came out, painting a vivid picture of our future and making me sick to my stomach.

Charlie rubbed his fingers across his jawline, his eyes heavy with the weight of the situation. "Let's not be dramatic..."

"I'm not being dramatic. Just realistic."

"Give her time—"

A knock sounded on our front door.

Charlie glanced at the entryway before he turned back to

me, his eyebrows raised slightly, silently asking if I was expecting company.

I shook my head as an answer.

"Maybe that's her." He walked to the front door, checked the peephole, and then opened it to reveal Dax on the other side.

I'd been hoping to see Kat come here to make amends after our fight, but this was a pleasant surprise too.

Dax didn't even look at Charlie as he came into the apartment and approached me.

I just wanted to be alone to lick my wounds in private, but seeing his handsome face, concern in his eyes, immediately made me feel better, like I didn't have to carry this alone, not anymore.

I moved into his body and wrapped my arms around his waist. My cheek planted against his chest, and I closed my eyes.

His powerful arms wrapped around me quickly, acting as my crutch so I wouldn't fall. He squeezed me tightly and showered me with affection, his lips moving to my forehead and then my hairline. "Sweetheart, I'm here."

"I know…" I never had to be alone again. I always had this man to comfort me, to carry my burden with me. It wasn't just me anymore, and hopefully it wouldn't be just me ever again. I completely let him in, let him see all of me, let him be a part of me. "I'm glad you came."

4

DAX

Carson lay beside me in bed, her body wrapped up in mine, her breathing deep and even now that she was calm.

I didn't ask for the details because they didn't matter.

She was sad. That was all I needed to know.

When she told me she wanted to be alone, I knew that was an impulsive response. If I'd really walked in the door, she would want me there. I had complete faith.

And I was right.

My fingers lightly played with her hair as we lay together under the sheets, the sound of traffic, honking horns, and loud ambulances passing in the street below. It was hard for me to sleep in her apartment when I could hear everything because I was used to the insulated silence of my penthouse. "Do you want to talk about it?"

"Not really."

"Okay."

"I just want to go to sleep...and leave this day behind." She pulled the sheets higher over her shoulder and came closer to me, no longer wanting her own space on the bed like she used to. She completely wrapped around me like we were one person.

"It'll get better, sweetheart. I know it's hard to believe, but it will."

The alarm went off the next morning, intrusively pulling us from our dreams.

She automatically reached across my body to grab my phone and quickly stabbed her fingers into the screen until the alarm shut off. Then she turned back over again, releasing a loud sigh of annoyance.

I watched her rub the sleep from her eyes and run her fingers through her hair, clearly having a rough time waking up.

I moved on top of her and pulled her thong down her legs until she was bare on the bottom. I dropped my boxers to settle between her legs, wanting to wake her up in a much better way than the obnoxious sound of the alarm clock.

Her eyes open slightly, and she released another sigh as I got into position, her hands gliding over my warm skin as her body automatically accepted mine.

I sank between her legs, feeling that slick wetness greeting me with the same enthusiasm as every other time. I pushed until I was deep inside her, our breaths both deep and labored, our minds slowly stirring at the feelings of pleasure.

I gave it to her slow and easy, just grinding against her, my face hovering above hers, watching her slowly become more enthused and feeling her body fully opening to me. Her arms moved under my shoulders, and her nails dug deep into my skin as she held on, gently rocking back with me as we made love first thing in the morning.

My arms were pinned behind her knees, and I barely moved my hips as I ground against her, being slow and gentle because we were both not quite awake enough for something aggressive. I was soaked in her arousal, squeezed by her tightness, and my breathing grew deeper and more ragged because it felt so good. Sex first thing in the morning was much better than a hot cup of coffee.

She came quietly, the only indication of her pleasure the way her nails dug into me, the tightness that increased around my length, and the water in her eyes.

I finished shortly afterward, giving her my entire desire, filling her tightness with my seed. The condoms had been abandoned and it was just the two of us, and goddamn, it felt right.

And the way she finally let me in made everything so much better.

We both groaned together as we finished, wanting to go back to sleep so we could wake up later and do it again.

"That was an improvement over the alarm clock…"

I kissed the corner of her mouth before I got out of bed and pulled on all my clothes.

She turned over like she was about to go back to sleep.

"Sweetheart."

She groaned loudly. "Ugh. It's the one time I wish I were a billionaire so I could just not go to work."

I left the bedroom and walked into the kitchen to have a cup of coffee.

Charlie was already there, standing at the counter with a steaming cup in front of him. He was looking through his phone when I joined him and poured two mugs of coffee.

One for me and one for my woman.

He slid his phone into his jeans then turned to me. "How is she?"

"Right this second? Really well."

He knew exactly what that meant and rolled his eyes.

I stood beside him and stared at his face, seeing the bags under his eyes, the tightness in his jaw. "She looks better than you do."

He rubbed his palm across his jawline, which was getting

thick with a beard because he'd skipped the shave a couple days in a row. "That doesn't surprise me."

"Did you sleep last night?"

"Not really."

I brought the mug to my lips and took a drink. "Carson didn't give me a lot of details, but it sounds like it didn't go well."

He shook his head.

"It'll work out. I know that probably doesn't make you feel better right now, but it will."

"I'm not worried about Denise. If Kat doesn't want to be friends with me anymore, I would understand that. But…I would feel like shit if Carson lost her best friend because of me."

"Wasn't that always a risk?" I asked before I took another drink.

"But it didn't seem likely. Unfortunately, Kat was angrier with Carson than she was with me, which isn't fair."

No wonder Carson was in such bad shape.

"I finally got what I want, but at what cost?" He took another drink of his coffee before dumping it out and placing the cup in the sink. "But it's nice to see the two of you so close. I'm not the one who needs to be there for her. Now it's you."

Renee put the various folders on my desk so I could go through them when I had a chance. "Here are all the numbers I pulled. I checked them three times, so they should be right."

"Thank you." I grabbed the first one and opened it, going over all the data she'd compiled for me. When I felt her stare on my face, I lifted my chin and looked at her. "Anything else, Renee?"

She beamed brighter than the sun.

"What?"

"You've been happy all week. Really happy."

I closed the folder and tossed it on the desk. "When people look happy, it usually means they are happy." I wasn't just happy that I was getting laid, but that Carson had completely opened up to me, had completely given me her trust.

"But you're consistently happy. Every day, you've got that smile on your face, and it never drops. It's really nice."

"Well, I'm sure you figured out the reason for my happiness."

"Yeah."

I grabbed my folder again and flipped through the pages. When Renee didn't walk away, I turned back to her. "Yes?"

This time, she looked different, definitely a lot more somber. "Rose is coming in tomorrow…"

We didn't deal with each other most of the time. She had an assistant who helped her with whatever she needed, but sometimes an interaction was unavoidable. "Whatever."

"I just hate how she walks in here like she owns the place."

"Well, she does own *half* the place." Because of my stupidity. Because I'd let her manipulate me like a goddamn idiot.

"There's got to be something we can do, some kind of loophole."

I shook my head. "Renee, I've spent a lot of time thinking about this, spent a lot of money for the best lawyers to think about this. If there were a way, I would've found it. Until she allows us to buy her out, we're stuck with her."

She released a heavy sigh, like the weight of the situation was just as much of a burden on her shoulders as it was on mine. "I told William if we get married, I need a prenup. Nothing personal. He understood."

"He seems like a guy who would."

"Who knew marriage was the most dangerous thing to a wealthy person?"

It really was, at least in a fifty-fifty community property state. "Can be. But if done right, I'm sure it's the happiest thing in the world. Don't let my mistake ruin the good things in your future, Renee."

She continued to stand over my desk and look at me. "Would you ever think about getting married again?"

If she'd asked me this before Carson, my answer would've been definitive.

Hell fucking no.

But now that we were officially together, both of our guards down, my answer had changed. "Yes."

She nodded slowly. "Good."

"It would be different with Carson." There was no doubt in my mind that she wanted me for me, not for any other reason. She seemed indifferent to my wealth, seemed to brush over the nice things I could offer her. Her brain simply wasn't wired that way, to focus on monetary gains instead of accomplishments. She wanted to change the world—not to be rich. She was a special kind of person. The idea of spending my life with somebody like her didn't seem so scary.

"Yeah, I think it would be too."

5

DAX

After I left the office, I joined the guys at the bar. The game was on, so we got together in an oversize booth to watch the screen.

Matt and Jeremy were already there, sitting close together, talking about the pads under the players' uniforms.

Nathan and Charlie walked in together at the same time.

After they each got a beer from the bar, they joined us. We made small talk about the game, threw out some wagers, and then enjoyed our beers and waited for the hot wings to come out.

Jeremy turned to Nathan. "How are things going with Kat?"

Nathan gave a slow shrug. "Pretty bad, I guess."

Charlie stilled at the response, his eyes shifting to Matt.

"What's that supposed to mean?" I asked. My hand grabbed the bottle, and I leaned against the leather padding in the booth as I stared at him.

Nathan looked down at his beer before he gave an answer. "She ended things yesterday. Just said it wasn't working. I didn't ask a lot of questions. We weren't serious anyway, so..." He gave another shrug.

"Are you okay?" Jeremy asked. "I know you aren't the commitment type, but you seemed to like her."

"I did." He took a drink of his beer. "But when somebody wants to break up, you break up. I have too much dignity to try to talk her out of it, you know?"

Charlie didn't participate in the conversation and instead stared down into his beer, as if this were another blow to his plan.

I wasn't sure why Kat would dump Nathan so unexpectedly, but I suspected it had something to do with Charlie and Carson. Maybe she didn't want to date a guy who was mutual friends with the people she never wanted to see again. Or maybe she realized she needed to find a guy she really liked so she could get over Charlie for good. Nathan just didn't fit the bill.

"I suggested that we be friends since we all hang out now," Nathan said. "She seemed fine with that."

Charlie released a quiet sigh beside me, likely suspecting that was bullshit.

The waitress brought out the hot wings. She handed out the plates, made small talk, and then turned to me. "You come in here a lot."

It took me a second to respond to her, because I was still immersed in the news I'd just received. I finally gathered my thoughts and addressed her. "Good beer. Good food. I'm a happy customer."

She chuckled as she slipped her hand into her apron and pulled out a napkin with her phone number written on it. She set it in front of me and walked away.

The guys all watched her go before turning back to me.

Her name was written on the napkin in pretty handwriting along with a :-). I slid it across the table to Nathan. "I think you can get more use out of this than I can."

Nathan folded up the napkin and put it in his pocket. "Sounds good to me."

"Wow." Jeremy shook his head as he looked at me across the table. "Dax Frawley is really off the market."

"Yep." I took a drink as I watched the TV. "And I hope I'm off the market for a really long time."

"Carson is pretty cool," Jeremy said. "But she seems to go back and forth a lot... Are you sure that's a good idea?"

Charlie got fired up immediately. "Excuse me? What exactly do you mean by that?"

I gave him an angry look across the table, silently telling him to keep his mouth shut.

"Nothing bad," Jeremy said quickly. "It just seemed like they had a lot of problems and Carson wasn't interested. Just don't want to watch my friend get smashed again."

"If he doesn't lie out of his ass again, we won't have any problems." Charlie raised his voice a little higher, growing more menacing.

The nice atmosphere had been demolished, and now it was just tense. I tried to smooth it over. "Jeremy is just looking out for me. He doesn't mean anything bad by what he said. But Carson and I are really happy. It took some time for us to get there, but we made it, and the destination was worth the journey."

That seemed to quiet everything down, so we went back to watching the game and eating the hot wings.

Charlie was the only one who still seemed angry, but I suspected it had nothing to do with us. He had a lot on his mind and shoulders—and it showed.

THE GUYS TOOK off after the game, so it was just Charlie and me. He'd had more beers than I had, either because his tolerance was somehow higher or he just didn't care right now.

"You seem down." I'd moved to the seat across from him

once the guys left. Since the game was over, there was no point in looking at the TV anymore.

"What gave me away?" Charlie said sarcastically.

"I'm sorry, man." It was unfortunate that I was happier than I'd ever been, but Carson and Charlie were dealing with this problem that weighed them both down.

He shook his head as he looked out the glass doors that showed the street. "I don't know what to do. Most of the time, exes just can't be friends, and I think Kat and I are an example of those kinds of exes. Losing her friendship permanently is a bit sad, but if she feels as strongly as she does...maybe it is best if we go our separate ways. I want her to find someone she really loves and be happy. But I really don't want Carson to lose her too. It wasn't her fault."

I thought Carson got the short stick in this cruel game. No matter what she did, she had her loyalty pulled in three different directions, every single person expecting something from her. Of course she couldn't live up to everyone's assumptions. She was a victim of a problem that was bigger than herself.

"And now Kat isn't seeing Nathan anymore... That's not a good sign."

"No."

He brought his beer to his lips. "We're all fucked." He took a drink. "How can I go after Denise when I'm in such a bad mood? I've wanted this for so long, and now it doesn't feel right."

"Because you feel guilty about Kat?"

"I guess I feel guilty about everything..." Charlie looked past me to the TV behind me. "I wish I had just stayed committed to Kat. Honestly, we were really happy. I wish Denise didn't affect me the way she does. My life would be far less complicated if that had never happened."

"Yeah, life can be cruel sometimes."

"You're telling me."

I didn't see Charlie as just Carson's friend, but my friend as well, and as years went by, I hoped we would become closer. That made me want to help him as much as I could. "What if you talked to Kat yourself?"

His eyes came back to me.

"You probably can't smooth over your problems with her, but maybe you can fix the situation between Kat and Carson. That's all you really care about, right?"

He nodded. "I just have a feeling she never wants to see me again."

Finding out most of your relationship was a complete lie would make anyone pull away.

"If I do that, I still need to wait a while. Let her cool off for a bit."

"Yeah, maybe you should."

He finished the last of his beer then glanced at the bar like he might order another, but something changed his mind. He left the empty bottle on the table. "Carson is finally happy with you, and I'm overshadowing it with my drama. I've wanted her to feel better for a long time now, and it finally happens, and then this shit goes down..."

"It'll get better." Carson hadn't been the same since all of this happened, and I missed the way it was the first weekend we'd had together in my penthouse. It was a dream, having her beside me all night, watching her want to stay with me instead of darting for the door right after sex or first thing in the morning. It was what I'd wanted since the beginning, to really be with her, to be happy.

"Yeah... I hope so."

"And she and I have the rest of our lives, so if it takes a while for this to resolve, that's fine."

He lifted his gaze and looked at me. "*The rest of our lives?* Look, don't get ahead of yourself like last time. Don't push anything too heavy. Just live in the moment with her and let her steer the ship."

My eyes narrowed. "She and I are in the same place, man." When I'd said those three little words to her, I was taking a huge risk. I knew it was more likely that it would scare her off instead of bring her closer, but she accepted those words with tears...and said them back. So I didn't know why Charlie had any doubts that Carson was ready to be in this relationship completely.

"She said that?" he asked incredulously.

My eyebrows rose in surprise because it seemed like he had no idea the feelings we had exchanged. I hadn't said it again and neither had she, but I suspected we would be one of those couples that only said it once in a while, not every time we got off the phone or departed from a room. She told him everything, but he seemed to have no idea about this. "I told her I loved her...she said it back."

His eyes snapped wide open like he couldn't believe the news. "Really? Carson?" Then his eyes narrowed in suspicion, and he rubbed his palm across his jawline. "That really happened?"

"Why would I lie about something like that?"

"I don't know. You lied about being a billionaire, so..."

I released a quiet chuckle because I would never live that down. "Yes. It happened the night we left the bar. She came over...and I told her." I wouldn't give him all the details because the intimacy was just for me. "She said it back. Rest is history."

Charlie was speechless now.

"She didn't tell you." For someone like Carson, who confided everything in this person, I was surprised she hadn't shared such a big moment with him.

He shook his head.

Maybe she thought it was just for us. Maybe we were so

special she didn't want to share us with anyone else. I decided not to jump to conclusions and take it as a compliment.

"Well, I'm really happy for both of you. I mean, I never thought Carson would get to this place, and it makes me happy that she has. Maybe someday, it can be the four of us…"

"Yeah. Maybe."

6

DAX

I'd become indifferent to Rose. I didn't spend my free time thinking about her. I never looked back and reflected on the relationship, second-guessing my decisions and mourning my mistakes. I made my peace with it and moved forward.

But whenever we were in the same room together...I hated her.

I *really* hated her.

I walked into the conference room and saw her sitting there with her lawyer at her side. Her blond hair was in soft curls over one shoulder, and she wore designer clothing she didn't pay for. She even had a level of pretentiousness she didn't earn, snobby like some trust-fund baby, when her beginnings were humble.

I was the one who gave her everything.

Without me, she'd be nothing.

Before we married, she was a regular person, working at a coffee shop for minimum wage.

When I'd asked her out, she took advantage of the opportunity—and ran with it.

Even if I could prove in a court of law that our entire relationship was a sham because she was an opportunistic parasite, it wouldn't change anything.

I didn't get that fucking prenup.

I took a seat across from her, beside Renee, along with a few other executives who worked at the company. We were going over quarterly figures.

That was why Rose was there.

She wanted to know what her paycheck was.

Splitting my income with her wasn't the worst part. Letting her take a piece of my family's legacy...that was what hurt.

We handed out the files and went over the numbers, business as usual.

I barely looked at her.

Whenever her stupid voice entered the conversation, I focused on the one thing that could calm me down.

Carson.

"It looks like you're spending a lot of money on research, doubling your budget from last month." Rose looked over the paperwork, acting like an executive even though she had no business experience at all. "I'm not sure if I approve of that."

Renee kept her head down and released a suppressed sigh, swallowing her insults because it would get us nowhere.

I steadied my anger and spoke. "We have to keep reinventing our company if we want to survive another generation. Companies that just sit back and do nothing never last. I assume that's the last thing you want...since you have nothing else."

She turned her blue eyes on me, her plump lips outlined with a racy color of lipstick. There was no guilt in her look, no second-guessing. She didn't give a damn what she did to me.

She owned it.

When the meeting was finished, she rose to her feet and strutted out. Her spike heels echoed against the hard floor as she walked out, her head held high as if she'd built this company from the ground up.

"Sometimes I want to jump over the table and break her neck." Renee put her papers in her folders, a bit of redness to her cheeks from her anger.

"Yeah...I know the feeling."

7

DAX

I sat on the couch in front of the TV and nursed my scotch. I usually went for a run after work, but today, I totally ditched the obligation because I just wanted to sulk in silence.

Carson texted me. *I had to stay late at the office today, so I'm just leaving now. Dinner?*

I wasn't in the mood to do anything right now. But I didn't want to push her away, do anything to jeopardize what we finally had. *I already ate. But you're welcome to come over.*

Alright. I'm picking up Chinese.

See you soon.

Thirty minutes later, my elevator beeped quietly before the doors opened, revealing Carson on the other side, wearing skinny jeans and green booties with a black sweater on top. A plastic bag of takeout was in her hand. "Hey, babe."

Did she just call me babe? "Hey, sweetheart." I got to my feet so I could greet her properly instead of letting my sour mood destroy the energy in the room.

Besides, it seemed like my night just got better.

My arms wrapped around her small waist, and I leaned down and gave her a kiss.

I was shirtless and in just my sweatpants, so her hand groped me dramatically without apology.

I smiled against her lips, letting her know I liked it when she made me feel desirable, made me feel I was worthy of her. I knew I was attractive, but I rarely got compliments from women, maybe because they thought my qualities were obvious and should go unsaid. But beautiful women liked to be complimented, and the same applied to men.

"I know you said you weren't hungry, but I got some extra spring rolls if you change your mind." She stepped back and shook the bag, the plastic film making a shimmering sound.

It was hard not to smile. "Thanks for thinking of me."

She carried the bag to the dining table behind the TV and ripped it open. "I'm sorry, but I'm starving." She went to the kitchen and grabbed a fork and then took a seat so she could eat her chow mein and sweet-and-sour chicken.

I grabbed my glass of scotch and took the seat beside her. I watched her devour her food, quickly shoveling it into her mouth like she hadn't eaten in days. "How was your day?"

It took a long time for her to give a response because there was always food in her mouth. "I've been doing a lot of surveillance today. Basically, stalking my prey."

"Who's the prey?"

"Pharmaceutical company that I can't name. I have information that they're purposely changing the concentrations of their drugs to make people sick. I've got to figure out what I'm going to threaten them with." She stabbed her fork into the food again and took a few more bites.

Her profession would always be difficult for me, knowing she was rattling cages and pissing off people she should avoid. It would always make me worry about her. There were times when I wanted to ask her to step aside for me, but I knew it would just make me lose her. If I wanted to keep her, I'd have to accept this part of her life. "And you've narrowed down your targets?"

"Yep." She dipped her spring roll into her dipping sauce and took a bite, the crunch audible. "How was your day?"

I shrugged. "Not my best day..."

"What happened?" She stopped eating like it was a limited-time buffet and gave me more of her attention, her eyes showing her sincere interest.

I shook my head. "Doesn't matter. Just wasn't good." I didn't want to spend time talking about my ex-wife, not when I was with the woman I should've been with in the first place. I used to believe everything happened for a reason, but now, I wasn't sure. What could possibly be the reason for me to marry someone who just used me? To make me so paranoid that I created a fake life to lie to Carson? It seemed like a lot of work.

"You don't have to talk about it if you don't want to. But I'm always happy to listen...if you change your mind."

That gave me a change of heart. If I wanted her to be open with me, I had to reciprocate. It wasn't that I felt uneasy sharing my life with her; I just didn't want to dampen what we had by talking about a woman who already took up enough of my time. "I had a meeting today at work, and *she* was there. She always brings her lawyer to these things, and her only interest is determining what her paycheck is for the quarter. She doesn't even have the class not to make it obvious. She questions my business decisions whenever it decreases her revenue, and I actually have to justify what I'm doing...*to* her."

Carson was silent as she continued to look at me, clearly searching for something comforting to say. She obviously didn't find anything because her only response was silence.

I looked out the window in front of us, seeing the city lights become brighter as the night intensified.

Her hand went to mine on the table, and her small fingers caressed my skin. "I'm sorry. I can't even imagine..."

"Yeah. Fucking sucks."

"But you don't have to see her a lot, right?"

I shook my head. "Thankfully."

She turned in her seat altogether, her knees hitting my chair. Her fingers remained in mine, her gentle pulse vibrating against my hand. "There's really nothing you can do?"

"Besides murder? No."

"I could beat her ass for you...if you want."

That immediately made me smile, not because I would actually ask her to do it, but I could clearly picture that scenario. Rose would step out of the building, and Carson would beat her ass right on the sidewalk. "No, it's okay."

"Offer is always on the table."

"No doubt." I turned my gaze away from the window and looked at her face, her glowing eyes. "I don't want to talk about her anymore. I'd rather spend all my time thinking about you."

"I'm not sure you want to do that."

"Why?"

"Well, if you think about me all the time, you're gonna be walking around with a big-ass boner, twenty-four seven."

That made me burst with a chuckle, and it made me immediately snap out of my bad mood too. "That's a valid point."

A beautiful smile formed on her face, like my happiness increased her own.

This was a new side to her that I wasn't used to quite yet. She'd always been beautiful, always been exceptional since the moment I'd laid eyes on her, but the softness was just exquisite. Her eyes were no longer guarded, her lips were always ready for my kiss, and she looked at me with her heart on her sleeve, like I was the only man she wanted to give herself to.

How did I get so lucky?

I knew it was a hard road to get here, but it was worth it every step of the way.

When my stare lingered for a long time, she asked, "What?"

I brought her hand to my lips and kissed her knuckles.

"Nothing." I moved her hand back to the table and continued to hold it.

I hadn't been looking for anything serious before this. If I'd never met her, maybe I always would've felt that way. But listening to her tell off that guy in the bar the night we met made me connect with her emotionally before even seeing her. I respected her fire, respected her for using it against an opponent. She was the kind of woman I'd been looking for without even knowing it. I hadn't even been divorced for a year then, but I felt like I was already ready for something great. "I'm just...in love with you."

She stilled at the admission, but she wasn't afraid, just deeply touched by the unexpected confession.

I didn't miss the one-night stands. I didn't miss the strip clubs. I didn't miss being single. I was never as happy then as I was now. Finding one incredible woman to be committed to with my entire soul was nirvana.

"I'm in love with you." She glanced down at our joined hands before she gave me a squeeze and looked back up, her eyes so soft and gentle.

I could stare at that beautiful face forever, look into those green eyes and never get bored. I pitied anyone who didn't have this. I actually pitied Rose because she was too evil to ever find this. She had half my money—but she didn't have this.

HER HAND CUPPED MY NECK, her fingers reaching into my hair. With her brown hair all over the place underneath her, she looked up at me with eyes bright like Christmas ornaments. When we were together, it wasn't about getting off, about only good sex, it was about being together, so her eyes were always on me, always soft, always pulling me directly into her heart.

Her legs were wrapped around my waist, ankles locked together against my lower back, and I slowly rocked into her, felt her so intimately that I could map out her body with my mind. She was always ready for me, always tight, always anxious. I breathed deeply with her, sometimes dipping my neck so I could kiss her collarbone or her shoulder. When we made love, I didn't just want her lips. I wanted her soft skin, her deep breaths, her bright eyes. My tongue wanted to taste her everywhere. I wanted to feel her heartbeat against my chest and have her feel mine.

I'd never felt more alive than when we were close like this, our bodies slowly moving together, high off the connection between our souls rather than the lust between our flesh.

Her hand slowly dragged down my chest, her claws out, and her thighs squeezed my hips tighter, like she was about to descend into pleasure. "Dax..." Her hand moved back to my neck, and she fisted my hair, gripping it tightly as her entire body began to writhe.

I started to thrust into her harder, grinding my body right against her clit so she could fall apart in ecstasy.

When she came, her nails nearly sliced into my skin, and she moaned uncontrollably into my face. Her mind went elsewhere as her body took over, riding the high that made all the neurons in her brain fry.

I thrust harder and harder, catching on to her coattails and descending with her, groaning in mutual pleasure, her body accepting what I gave her.

It was so fucking good.

Damn.

When we finished, we were still two single bodies wrapped together, still two people who didn't want to break apart.

If sleep weren't essential to function, I would skip it and just keep doing this—all night long.

I moved off her and lay on the bed beside her, feeling the

sweat start to evaporate from my body the second we broke apart. The heat from our mutual desire faded as soon as we were finished, and the room felt cold.

She didn't get up to go the bathroom. She closed her eyes and took advantage of all the good chemicals that had released in her brain so she could drift off to sleep.

I lay beside her and stared at her, the most beautiful woman in the world in my bed. I was so used to sleeping with her at this point that it was hard to sleep without her. There were some nights a week when we were apart—and it never felt right.

The only time the world felt right was when she was with me.

8

DAX

We warmed up on the court and passed the ball around to make our shots. We were already sweaty with our hearts pumping before the game even began.

I noticed Carson and Charlie walk through the double doors and join us, both with towels over their shoulders and water bottles in their hands. They were talking to each other, engaged in conversation.

Carson was in a pair of little black shorts and a blue tank top, the color beautiful on her. She had the nicest legs, perkiest ass, and when her hair was pulled back from her face, it showed just how beautiful she was—without makeup.

They took a seat on one of the benches and continued their conversation.

I broke away from the guys and joined them. "Hey, sweetheart."

Carson rose to her feet, a breathtaking smile entering her lips, and she greeted me with a kiss that was *not* rated PG-13. Her hand went to my bare stomach, and she gripped my strong abs. "Hey, babe."

I gave her ass a tight squeeze before I pulled away. "I like it when you call me that."

"Yeah?" she asked. "I like it when you grab my ass like that."

"I already knew that." I winked before I greeted Charlie with a handshake. "Hey, man."

He returned the gesture and gave me a nod. "Ready to lose again?"

"I don't plan on losing today."

"Well, Carson is pretty fired up, so you don't have much of a chance." Charlie took a drink from his water bottle.

I turned back to Carson. "I know how to keep her distracted..."

"Give me your best shot." She started to saunter onto the court.

I smacked her ass as she walked away before I turned back to Charlie. "Where's Matt?"

Charlie turned to look at the entryway just as Matt and Denise walked inside. "They got into an argument and fell behind."

"An argument about what?"

"NSYNC or Backstreet Boys."

I chuckled. "Aren't they old?"

"Well, then it segued into a discussion about One Direction... I don't think Matt will be able to focus now." He turned to look at Denise as she came closer, wearing a long-sleeved dress and boots. He gave a really deep sigh before he turned back to me. "I don't think I will either." He stripped off his shirt and joined us on the court. Matt took a little longer.

Charlie shouted back at him. "Get your ass out here!"

Matt walked onto the court and turned around to shout back at Denise once more. "You know Harry carried the whole band! Don't even lie." He put up his hand to silence her before he joined us in the middle of the court. "She has terrible taste."

Carson stood with her hands on her hips, stretching her core. "You're so red in the face I would assume you were talking about politics."

"Politics?" Matt asked incredulously. "No one cares about politics. People care about the best boy band in history. That's what matters."

"Are we gonna play?" Charlie asked. "Or have a debate about the hottest member of the band?"

"Hey." Matt pointed at him. "I'm trying to establish some girl talk so I can see what she says about you. So, shut your mouth." He dropped his hand. "And you know that's JT. Come on."

"If Charlie wanted to know, I could just ask her," Carson said.

"That's not girl talk," Matt countered. "Talking to your sister is not real girl talk. Talking to a handsome and sophisticated gay man is."

I liked my friends and never took them for granted, but Carson and her gang were always interesting. "Let's get this game started so I can grope my girlfriend." I looked at Carson and waggled my eyebrows.

She rolled her eyes like what I'd said was stupid, but I knew she loved it.

"Alright." Matt stood in the middle with the ball. "Let's get the jump shot going and get this party started."

AT THE END of the game, we walked to the bleachers and wiped down with our towels. Water was squirted into our mouths, and we caught our breath. It had been a competitive match, and I'd managed to distract Carson enough to make them lose.

It was a weak victory, but it was still a victory.

"You totally cheated." She stabbed her finger into my side to tickle me. "How am I supposed to get the ball when I have two enormous hands gripping my ass cheeks like that?"

"Oh, I don't know. You went to Harvard, so I'm sure you

can figure it out." Nothing got under her skin more than mentioning her alma mater, and when the irritated expression came over her face, I knew I'd accomplished exactly what I wanted.

She gave me a playful smack on the arm before she grabbed her water bottle.

"You guys are cute." Denise sat on the bleachers by herself, not looking at Charlie even though he was shirtless beside her, wiping down his sweaty body with a towel.

"You think this man sabotaging the game is cute?" Carson asked. "I think he's a punk."

I was so absorbed in Carson that I didn't notice the basketball aimed right for me. It came from my side and hit me before it fell to the floor and bounced away.

"Sorry!" A group of women high up on the bleachers waved at me. Their leader was a brunette in her workout clothes, a sports bra and leggings.

"It's no problem. Just an accident." I went after the ball and picked it up, and when I rose to my full height, the brunette was right in front of me, giving me a flirtatious attitude. "Here you go." I handed the ball back.

She took it and tucked it under her arm. "Can we play with you guys sometime? We aren't as good as you, but maybe you can give us a few pointers?"

Now I wondered if they'd thrown the ball at me on purpose just to get my attention. Was it not obvious I was with Carson? Instead of blowing the woman off right away, I thought the guys might like the opportunity to talk to the girls, so I said, "Maybe we—"

"Bitch, he's taken." Carson came to my side and stared down the girl trying to make a pass at me. "And don't act like you didn't know, because you did. Throw the ball at my man again, and I will shove that ball up your ass."

All her confidence disappeared, and she quickly turned away like a dog with its tail tucked between its legs.

Carson grabbed me by the wrist and pulled me back to the gang. "Let's go eat. I'm starving." As if nothing had happened, she dragged me away and groped my ass for the girls to see.

"You were a little harsh with that girl," Denise said across from her sister as she picked at her salad. The rest of us had pizza, wings, beer, but she chose to stick to something clean.

Carson was the same size, but she seemed to eat whatever she wanted. Right now, she had two slices of pizza on her plate along with a stack of extra hot wings. "Was not."

"I'm sure Dax gets hit on all the time," Denise said. "Are you gonna hunt them all down and call them bitches too?"

Carson continued to converse with her sister like I wasn't sitting right beside her. "Yes, of course, I know he gets hit on all the time. Look at the guy." She pointed at me with her thumb and gave me a once-over. "But she knew he was with me, and she thought she was hotter in her little workout outfit, so she went for it. She's a bitch, and she knows she's a bitch. I tell it how it is."

"If she knew and did it anyway, then yeah, that is pretty bitchy." Denise grabbed her root beer and took a drink.

"I don't feel bad." Carson picked up a wing and took a huge bite out of it. Then she chewed it for a long time in order to get it down her throat. "Come after my man, and I'll come after you."

I wiped my mouth with a napkin before I spoke. "I thought it was pretty hot...honestly."

"See?" Carson pointed at me. "He thought she was a bitch, too."

"Whoa, I did *not* say that." I wasn't walking around calling women bitches. My balls would be sliced off. "Just thought it was hot that you got jealous and did something about it."

Carson gave me a wink. "Good answer, babe."

"What if she tried to fight you?" Matt asked, his mouth full of food.

"I would beat her ass," Carson said. "She's one of those girls that spends a ton of money on her workout clothes but doesn't actually work out. It wouldn't even be a fair fight."

Charlie wiped his mouth with a napkin before he took a drink of his beer. "My money's on Carson. Always."

Carson blew him a kiss and whispered, "Love you."

He waved away her kiss like he was disgusted and didn't say it back.

I chuckled at their interaction, liking the way Charlie loved her like a sister, putting her down most of the time without wearing his heart on his sleeve. I wasn't the least bit worried that there was more to the relationship than met the eye.

"So..." Charlie wiped his fingers with a napkin, getting the hot sauce off his skin. "You're going to a fancy party on Saturday. Maybe you should take an etiquette course."

"Oh, shut up." She was hunched over her food as she bit into a greasy slice of pizza, the cheese stretching between her lips and the food, making a mess all over her hands and face. She finished the bite and said, "I'm fine."

Charlie gave her a blank stare as if he couldn't disagree more. "You should look in the mirror, kid. You look like a bear that found the honey stash."

"Well, I don't eat like this at nice places. And how are you supposed to eat pizza and hot wings without putting your elbows on the table and getting shit all over your face?" Carson asked defensively. "I'll be fine."

I hated the stuffy universe that contained my existence. Carson's realism was a breath of fresh air. Even if she did act like this on Saturday, I wouldn't care. "I don't care how she eats."

Carson turned to me and blew me a kiss before whispering, "Love you, babe."

I smiled. "Love you too."

She went back to eating.

Everyone stilled when they heard us exchange such heartfelt words, even if we were just making a joke.

"Besides," I said. "If she eats dirty, she does other things dirty too."

Denise cringed. "Ew."

Charlie immediately shifted his position in the chair like he was uncomfortable. "Okay now..."

Matt loved it. "Hell yeah." Then he proceeded to stare at me as if he was picturing me being the one to do the dirty things.

Carson wiped her face with her napkin before she leaned in to kiss me. "Aren't we just perfect together?"

I smiled as I slowly leaned in and gave her a kiss, my heart filling with so much love for this woman. It felt right; it felt true. We were like two magnets that came together and never broke apart. "Yeah." I rubbed my nose against hers before I pulled away. "We are."

She straightened in her chair and dunked her hot wing in a pool of ranch.

I continued to stare at her, no longer interested in my food.

"Do you have something to wear?" Denise asked.

"I have a couple black dresses that will do just fine," Carson said. "And I have Mom's earrings. Everyone else might be wearing designer gowns and stuff, but whatever." She turned back to me. "Is that okay?"

I would offer to buy her something nice, but it would turn into a fight I didn't want to have. So I just accepted whatever she had on hand. "As long as it's short and slutty, yes."

"It's backless." Carson smiled at me as she waited for my reaction.

My eyes stayed on her. "Even better."

9

CARSON

I LOOKED IN THE MIRROR ON THE WALL TO MAKE SURE MY earrings were correctly inserted into my lobes, and then I turned around to look at Charlie as he sat on the couch. "So, what do you think?" I struck a few poses, acting like Madonna from "Vogue."

His eyes barely glanced at me before they were back on the TV. "You look fine."

"*Fine?*" I asked incredulously. "That's all you're giving me? Like, fine, as in just alright? Or more like, damn, that bitch looks *fiiiiine*."

He considered it with a shrug. "The first one."

I rolled my eyes and left the living room, my heels starting to tap on the hardwood floor after I stepped off the rug.

"Nervous?" Charlie asked from the couch, his back to me.

I threw my head back and laughed loudly, like a villain that had the perfect plan to steal the vault of diamonds. "Oh, you're so funny."

Charlie got off the couch and turned to look at me. "I'm sure this is going to be fancy as fuck, a bunch of pretentious rich people talking about yachts. It might be intimidating."

"Intimidating?" I rolled my eyes. "A few trust-fund babies

don't intimidate me. If the mob makes me laugh, what will these guys do?" I opened my clutch and made sure all my valuables were there, including my phone since I had no pockets or anything in which to put my stuff.

Charlie joined me at the dining table and looked at me as he crossed his arms over his chest. "You look nice."

"Thank you. I want to look classy and like I belong there, but I also want Dax to pull me into a dark alleyway and fuck me like a whore. Just trying to set the perfect tone for that."

He chuckled. "So, you want to look like a classy whore?"

I rubbed my lips together as I considered it. "Yeah, pretty much. So, what are your plans for the night?"

He shook his head.

"Nothing?"

"I might order a pizza."

"Interesting..."

"Interesting, how? I recognize that tone."

"I just thought you would have gone for Denise by now. I'm going to be out of the apartment until tomorrow but probably Monday. Might be a good time to invite her over..."

Instead of jumping at the opportunity, he looked forlorn. "Doesn't feel like the right time."

"Because of Kat?"

He nodded. "I was hoping she would understand and give her blessing, and that would be it."

I released a burst of laughter. "Wow...that didn't happen at all."

"Yeah. I know."

"Well, I think we both put everything on the line so you could have what you wanted, so the whole thing would be pointless if you didn't, you know? The damage is done. Whatever happens...happens."

He shrugged. "Yeah. I guess."

Dax was supposed to pick me up any minute, so I continued to wait for his knock at the door. I'd curled my hair even though I usually left it straight, and I'd even put on fake lashes for this event. I never wore my makeup this heavy or donned my finest jewelry to impress anyone. I looked totally different from how I did any other day.

"Dax told me you guys did that *I love you* thing." There was a slight tone of accusation to his voice.

"Yeah, we did."

"I'm surprised you didn't tell me."

My only response was a shrug. I looked down at my black clutch in my hand as I remembered that evening.

"I'm happy for you."

"I know you are, Charlie." I lifted my gaze and looked at him again. "I've never been this happy in my life. I want to say I regret the way I acted before, regret the way he lied to me, but I can't. Because all those experiences brought us together and gave us this foundation."

"I wouldn't regret it either. You guys are perfect together. Two pieces of a puzzle."

"I think so too."

"Do you think you'll move in with him?"

"I don't know about that...it's not like we talked about it. Why do you ask?"

"Well, you always run to me to tell me everything. The fact that you kept this to yourself makes me realize he's becoming your home base. I'm being replaced. It's not a bad thing...but it's happening."

Now, I went to Dax with my problems. Now, I kept our quiet moments private because it belonged to us and not my friends. Our lustful relationship turned into something deep and meaningful. "You can never be replaced, Charlie. And yes, I know what you mean. If we moved in together, that would mean leaving this place and going to a penthouse—and that would be weird."

He chuckled. "Yeah, I can't picture you in that environment at all. Tell him to get an apartment with you."

"He would never do that. How can you go from the top to the bottom?"

"I have no doubt he would give up anything for you."

A soft smile moved onto my lips. "Yeah, you're right. But let's not get ahead of ourselves here. I have to go meet his rich friends first. Hope I don't stick my foot in my mouth…"

"Oh, I'm sure you will." He gave me an affectionate look.

Dax knocked on the front door.

"Looks like your knight in shining armor is here." Charlie stared at the door.

"Psh." I waved my hand in the air and snapped my fingers. "I don't need a knight. All I need is my shoe." I walked to the front door and straightened my posture before I opened it.

Dax stood there in a black tuxedo with a freshly shaved jawline. His hair was combed back, and he looked just as sexy as always. His eyes dropped down as he looked me over in my little black dress. A quiet whistle came from his lips the farther down he went. "Damn, you look fine."

A smile crept onto my features because it was the reaction I'd been looking for; I'd just been looking for it from the wrong person. "Thanks." I wanted to grab the front of his suit and pull him into me, but I didn't want to wrinkle his pressed clothing, so I moved into him and kissed him.

His hands automatically squeezed my ass.

When I pulled away, I saw Charlie was looking in the fridge, like he was trying to find something to stare at instead of us. "Now that's how you compliment a lady."

Charlie didn't turn around. "You're a lady?"

"Oh, shut it."

"Ready to go?" Dax asked.

"Yeah."

Dax looked around as if he expected me to bring something. "Where's your bag?"

I held up my clutch. "No big purse for this."

"I meant your overnight bag. I was hoping you would stay with me for the weekend."

"Oh..." I nodded in understanding. "I just figured we're not gonna wear any clothes or go anywhere, and I could always use your toothbrush, so...do I really need anything?"

The affection in his eyes matched his handsome smile, and he visibly melted right before my eyes.

"And I don't care about doing the walk of shame. I own that shit."

His arms wrapped around me, and he kissed me again, this time harder, like wanted to skip the dinner and just go home instead. "I love you."

Every time he said it, I couldn't just hear it, but feel it, feel it in the energy around us. His beating heart was safe inside his chest, but I could see it clearly, see it thudding through the skin. He was sincere and harmless, the kind of man that would never hurt me. "I love you too."

THE CHARITY PARTY was held at the Four Seasons. It was just as pretentious and stuffy as I'd imagined it would be, all the women wearing gowns, flutes of champagne being carried on trays, along with fancy hors d'oeuvres. Dax kept his arm around my waist as he guided me around and mingled with people. I was on my best behavior, acting like a classy woman who belonged there. I wasn't ashamed of who I was, but I didn't want to embarrass Dax with my bluntness.

I knew he liked me for who I was, but not everyone felt that way. Sometimes I was described as a lawless bitch.

It was fine. Took it as a compliment.

We eventually found Renee and William, and it was nice to see two familiar faces.

William leaned in and embraced me. "You look lovely."

He was such a kind man, the kind who could compliment a woman without seeming sleazy.

"Thanks. You too."

Renee hugged me next and gave me a fake kiss on the cheek. "My brother has been really happy lately. Always smiling. Always in a good mood. I know you have something to do with that."

Dax immediately sighed in embarrassment. "Could you not share everything with her?"

"I think it's cute." I moved closer into his side and hooked my arm through his. "I'm happy too, you know."

He leaned down and kissed me. He didn't have to bend his neck down when I was in these sky-high heels, so that made embracing much easier.

We moved farther along until we met his circle of friends. I recognized them from a mile away, not because I knew what they looked like, but because I could tell by their behavior that they were a bunch of rich playboys. For one, they were all drinking scotch or gin, when everyone else was enjoying champagne and wine. Two, their eyes constantly wandered, and they spoke louder than most people, talking about money and even women.

I couldn't picture Dax hanging out with these types of men, but at the same time, I could.

When Dax walked up, they greeted him with pats on the arm and back.

Dax made the introductions. "These are some of my boys. Clint, Joel, and Brad." He turned back to his friends, "Guys, this is the woman I told you about."

"Nice to meet you all," I said politely. "I've heard a bit about the parties and the strip clubs."

Clint smiled, clearly one of the arrogant ones. "And let me guess, Dax won't be joining us for those events anymore, now that he has you."

"I don't tell him what to do. If he tried to tell me what to do, that shit wouldn't last." I was a wild horse that couldn't be saddled, so I would never cross that line and manage Dax's life. If he wanted to go out and party, so be it. I was secure in our relationship, and I knew he would always be faithful.

Clint raised his eyebrows and looked impressed. "Wow, it just got hot in here because she brought the fire."

"Oh honey, you have no idea." These guys didn't intimidate me; their looks and money meant nothing to me. People were always surprised that I could step into a world where I didn't belong and thrive. It was because I knew nobody was better than me.

Clint released a laugh before he took a drink of scotch. "Now I'm understanding your fascination a little better."

Dax returned his arm around my waist. "Oh honey, that was just the opening act. Wait until you see everything she can do."

We sat at the table with his friends, while his sister and William sat elsewhere. The guys were exactly what I assumed them to be, a bunch of rich manwhores.

"So, we're at my place in the Hamptons, and she's bent over the bed, right?" Clint shared every detail of his life with Dax without a filter.

Dax raised his hand and interrupted him. "Maybe we can tone it down a bit?"

"I hope it's not for my sake," I said from Dax's other side. "It doesn't bother me."

Clint gave me a nod of approval before he continued. "So, I'm ramming her from behind, everything's great, and the doorbell keeps ringing and ringing... It won't stop. So, I have to pause what I'm doing and go downstairs. Guess who was at the door?"

Dax shrugged.

"Jessica. The lingerie model I was seeing. Apparently, I'd invited her up for the weekend when I was drunk off my ass and totally forgot."

Dax shook his head but seemed slightly amused.

"You know what happened then?" Clint said. "Jessica yelled at me for a bit, but I'm such a smooth talker that I ended up fucking both of them that night—side by side." He raised his fist in the air. "Who's the man?"

Dax shrugged. "Would have to be you."

"But you're the man, too," Clint said as he lowered his voice. "It wasn't that long ago that you—"

Dax quickly interrupted him. "Come on, Clint." He didn't raise his voice, but he definitely turned a little angry. "Don't do that shit."

No, I didn't want to picture Dax with other women or imagine the wild sex he had as a playboy in Manhattan, but I also saw that as his past, not his present. "Babe."

It took him a long time to turn back to me, as if he dreaded it.

My arm hooked around his shoulders, and I leaned into him, my hand moving over his thigh. "I don't care who was there before me. We both know none of them could compare to me anyway." I pressed a kiss to the corner of his mouth before I rose from the chair and headed to the restroom.

When I was still within earshot, I heard Clint say, "Damn. You've got one hell of a woman on your hands."

The pride in Dax's voice was unmistakable. "I know."

I crossed the room and headed to where the restrooms were located. There were a lot of people mingling, up from their seats and away from the tables, catching up with other socialites. I tried to get through a group of people talking, but that was a dead end, so I took another route around.

Then halted when I walked right up to somebody I knew.

Simon Prescott.

CEO of Kerosene Pharmaceuticals.

THE MAN I THOUGHT I TRUSTED   79

Aka, my new nemesis.

He was young, probably younger than thirty-five, definitely not a typical CEO, who were usually in their sixties.

He gave me a smirk like he recognized me. "I know who you are."

I'd always been quick on my feet, so I fired back. "And I know exactly who you are. Small world, huh?"

He stood with his hands in his pockets, standing tall in his tuxedo. "I know you've been trailing me everywhere I go. You journalists are all the same. But I can't say the reporters ever took it this far..."

"Well, you haven't dealt with a journalist like me." It was a complete coincidence that we were there at the same time, but it would make me look stupid to say that, so I played it cool.

"You're right. Maybe I underestimated you."

I shook my head and clicked my tongue. "Big mistake. I take down all the big bad wolves all over town, and it looks like you're next."

"Or maybe I should stop underestimating you and eliminate you."

I'd heard every threat in the book, and I never blinked an eye. Wasn't about to start now. "You know how many times I've heard that?"

"A lot," he said quietly, his eyes hardly blinking as he stared at me. "But this will be the last time you do." The guy was creepier than most of the villains I dealt with because he was calm and confident. My back talk got most guys fired up and they lost their cool, but this man kept his composure so easily. He was pragmatic, and logical people were usually smart. "You've got a good track record. Be proud of that all you want, but this is territory you don't want to step into. I'm not a murderer by trade, but if you keep pressing...you'll leave me no choice."

"Killing sick people is so important that you would kill another innocent person just to keep making sick people sicker? For money?" It was so disgusting that I could barely get the words out. I'd seen a lot of bad shit, but this was really gross. Bad men went after other bad men. It was nothing personal. But this was different because his company went after people who were weak, in pain, and sick.

He shrugged. "What's one more corpse added to the pile?" He started to walk away, his hands still in his pockets. "You're young and beautiful. Don't waste that fighting something you can't change." He walked away and disappeared into the crowd.

I didn't want to admit that he got under my skin, but he did. I headed to the restroom as I planned, but I continued to replay the conversation in my mind.

I'd locked up some of the biggest con men in history, traveled the world, and interacted with international terrorists, but there was something different about this guy.

Something very unusual.

"Why are you calling me?" Charlie asked over the phone.

I stood in the hallway away from the restrooms, speaking freely because there was nobody around. "Guess who I just ran into."

"I don't know…Arnold Schwarzenegger? Seriously, why are you calling me right now? Don't ditch Dax to gossip with me."

"He's a grown-ass man who can take care of himself. And no, not fucking Arnold Schwarzenegger, you idiot. Simon Prescott."

There was a long pause on the line. "Did he say anything to you?"

"Walked right up to me and said he knew I was tailing him."

"Shit, that's not good."

"He's a creepy guy."

"Aren't they all?"

"No. This guy is different... I can't explain it. He's really calm, soft-spoken, not the least bit put off by my existence. All the other guys get huffy and puffy and panicked in some way. But not this guy."

"What are you gonna do?"

"What do you mean? I'm doing the article. I'm never not completing my job."

"But if you're scared—"

"I'm not scared." I kept the phone to my ear and looked down the hallway to make sure nobody was coming. "I just think this guy is a strange breed, is all."

"Did he follow you tonight to provoke you?"

"No. He thinks I followed him—and crossed the line."

"Did you tell him it was a coincidence?"

"Absolutely not. That would make me look stupid."

"But the fact that you really caught him off guard makes you look like a serious threat now."

"Which is true. I am a serious threat."

He sighed into the phone. "I admire your grit. No one else has it like you do. Just remember, there's no article, no story, no praise that is worth losing your life. If this is more than you can handle, there's no shame in handing the article back to Vince."

I would never live with that kind of shame, default like a coward. I'd had to prove myself to get that spot at the paper, and I wasn't going to blow it now. "It's fine. It just means I have to move quicker than I wanted to."

"How are you going to get anywhere when he knows you're on to him?"

"It'll be harder, but that won't stop me." I glanced down the hallway and saw Dax heading my way, a look of concern in his eyes because I hadn't returned from the restroom after so long. "I gotta go. Dax is coming."

"We'll talk later." Charlie hung up.

I put the phone back in my clutch and closed it. "Hey, sorry I took so long."

He walked up to me, and his hands immediately slid over my hips. "Everything alright? You've been gone for almost thirty minutes."

"No, I'm totally fine. I had to call Charlie." I tucked my clutch under my arm and then grabbed Dax's hand so we could walk back together.

"And why did you have to call him?"

"A work thing. Don't worry about it."

"I don't know if I can. I've never seen you step aside to call Charlie like that. What happened?"

"I just saw one of the subjects of an article I'm working on. That's all."

He held my hand as he looked at me, his expression subtle, but his concern obvious. "You mean from the pharmaceutical article?"

"Yeah. I saw him. We exchanged words..."

"What kind of words?"

I totally played it down so he wouldn't worry. "You know, the usual. I'm not gonna find enough dirt to lock him up even though we both know I will... Same old shit."

He released a quiet sigh, like he was trying to swallow the words in his throat.

"Let's go back to your friends and talk about all those bitches and models."

He sighed again, but this time for a different reason. "I'm sorry Clint said that—"

"I'm not mad. Chill."

"When you didn't come back, I was worried that his words got under your skin."

I shook my head. "Not at all. I know what rich and handsome men do in their spare time, so it's not like I was surprised. And I know we're different, so what does it matter?"

He looked ahead as we continued to walk into the ballroom and approach our table. "I've got to be honest... If I had to listen to Charlie talk about your old lovers, I don't think I'd like it."

"I don't see why it should bother you. They were meaningless. And I'm in love with you, so..."

He stopped and pulled his hand away from mine. He turned to look at me, to look into my eyes with that absorbing gaze.

"Those women meant nothing to you, so why should I care? Why be jealous of them when they should be jealous of us?" I rose slightly on my heels and kissed him on the mouth. "Now, let's sit down. I've been waiting for that dessert all night..."

WHEN WE GOT BACK to his penthouse, there was no gentle undressing, no quiet whispers of love and devotion.

He positioned me on all fours on the edge of his bed and yanked up my dress. The only thing that came off was my thong. The heels remained on my feet.

His jacket and bow tie were on the floor, his collared shirt open, and his slacks rested on his hips as he pulled down his boxers and let his hard cock spring free.

He shoved himself inside me, every inch of that fat length hitting me hard.

"Oh god..."

He got a good grip on my hair and tugged my head back so my face was tilted toward the ceiling. One hand was on my hip, and then he went to town.

He fucked me like I meant nothing to him.

And I loved it.

With my heels over the edge and my back arched, I took his entire length over and over, feeling him slam into my wet flesh again and again. I looked out the window at the city, seeing his faint reflection in the glass. I could see his tanned skin through the opening in his shirt, see the tightness of his jawline as he clenched his teeth.

It was so hot.

He gripped the back of my neck and shoved my face down into the bed, raising my ass in the air even more. Then he scooted a little closer and fucked me harder.

My hands reached behind me to grip his thighs as I lay there and took it, moaning into the sheets as tears dripped from the corners of my eyes and soaked into the fabric.

He grunted through his thrusts. "Fuck, I love this pussy." He grunted again, slamming his length inside until he was balls deep. "Jesus fucking Christ."

He wasn't just good in bed, but listening to him verbally desire me, talk dirty like that, was such a turn-on. It made me come a moment later, feeling that big dick ram into me, even though there was nowhere for it to go. "God...yes."

When he felt me come around his length, he joined me, moaning as he flooded me with his come. "Fuck." His strokes slowed down as he filled me.

I loved feeling his heaviness every time we were finished. It was much better than the condoms, to feel my man's desire right between my legs.

He slowly pulled out of me and gave my ass a hard smack with his hand.

I groaned at the hit, feeling the burn in my cheek from his palm. I rolled over onto my back.

He was still standing there, his dick still hard. He grabbed on to my hips and dragged me to the edge before he shoved himself inside me again, moaning like he hadn't just filled me seconds ago. He moved through my come and his and fucked me all over again. "Damn."

"Could you wash the broccoli?" Dax stood at the kitchen counter and sliced the meat into strips so he could throw it into the hot pan.

I stood there and watched him prepare his own food instead of paying a chef to do it.

Dax stopped slicing and turned to look at me. "Sweetheart?"

When I heard his question, I met his look. "Sorry, what?"

"Could you wash the broccoli?"

"Yeah, sure thing." I wore his t-shirt and walked to the fridge and grabbed the florets. Then I rinsed them under the sink before I patted them dry.

Dax returned to his food prep. "What were you thinking about?"

My eyes were on my hands as I handled the vegetables. "Just work..."

"About that guy you saw last night?"

That was exactly who I was thinking about. "Just my article and stuff like that."

"I've never seen you distracted before."

"Well, it happens." When the broccoli was dry, I threw it into the other pan and added salt and pepper.

When he was done with his task, he placed the chicken in the pan, and it really began to sizzle. Now, there was nothing to do except wait, so he leaned against the counter and looked at me.

I'd washed off my makeup because it was better to have no makeup than shitty makeup. My hair was still curled from the night before, but by tomorrow, it would be straight again. "It already smells good."

He continued to watch me with that dark stare, like he was the one who was distracted now. He crossed his arms over his chest.

I felt like I was being interrogated with silence instead of words. "What?"

"I wasn't going to say anything, but I worry about you."

"What did I do to make you so worried about me?" I met his concern with coldness, because I didn't need someone to worry about me.

"Don't do that."

"Do what?"

"Blow me off. Push me away. We've made so much progress, so don't start this shit now. I'm in love with you, and I have every right to worry about you."

I held his gaze for a few seconds before I looked at the food on the stove. I grabbed the spatula and stirred things around before I looked at him again.

"I know you share those stories with a comical slant, but I also know that's not how they really play out. I know you're dealing with the head of a big corporation that probably has ties that go deep underground. Whatever happened was big enough for you to call Charlie in the middle of an event."

"I was just excited. You're reading too much into it."

"I was there when some guy tried to hurt you in an alleyway. What if I hadn't been there?"

"I would've gotten away. I always get away."

His tone deepened. "Doesn't mean you'll *always* get away. I don't like this. I'll never tell you what to do, but this scares me."

I didn't want to deal with this right now. We'd just gotten together, and now we had another obstacle to face. "Dax, please don't."

"I have to. I love you."

"Look, we're finally together, and we're finally happy. Can we not ruin that by having a serious conversation about my job? I love my job and I'm not gonna stop doing it, so this conversation is pointless. Please don't sabotage what we have."

"I'm not sabotaging anything." His dark eyes burned into mine like he was truly upset but doing his best to suppress it.

"I care about you. A lot. I'm going to keep caring about you, so this is going to come up."

"Then let's worry about it later."

He shook his head. "You can worry about it later, but I'll always worry about it. I know you're strong and smart, but you can't win every battle. I know I'm getting ahead of myself right now, but I want you to be my wife and I want to have kids. How is that going to work with us?"

We hadn't talked that far into the future, but hearing him admit so candidly that he wanted forever with me, that he wasn't afraid of commitment, that he wanted to have a family with me, touched me…deeply. "Let's worry about it later."

"Carson—"

"Later." I pushed off the counter and walked toward him, knowing the broccoli was turning black because it was already burned. "It took so long for us to come back together, let's not jeopardize that over something else. Let's just be happy…at least for now."

His hands automatically moved to my waist as he stared down at me, conflict in his eyes.

I knew it wasn't out of line for him to worry about me, especially when a man had threatened to kill me in the middle of a crowded room. But my job was everything to me, and I didn't want to walk away from it.

It took him a few seconds to calm down, but when he did, he came back to reality, came back to the moment. "Okay. For now."

10

CARSON

Lately, I hadn't mentioned Kat much to either Charlie or Dax, but that didn't mean the situation wasn't on my mind. I usually thought about it right before I went to sleep and sometimes during breaks throughout the day.

I hoped that with enough time, Kat would come around... but she was still radio silent.

I decided to wait on the sidewalk outside her office for her to leave work. It was a cold afternoon, so I got two hot coffees and waited.

She opened the glass doors and emerged onto the sidewalk, wearing thigh-high boots and a long-sleeved sweater dress. It took her a moment to notice me.

I stood there with the coffees in my hand, and I tried to think of something witty to say, something to break the ice and make her laugh. But I couldn't think of anything.

She looked like I'd just ruined her day. She turned around and walked the other way.

"Kat." I tossed the coffees into the garbage can and caught up to her. "Come on, just talk to me."

She turned back around and looked at me. "Talk about what? I'm pretty sure we said everything that needs to be said."

It hurt me so deeply to see how much she despised me, how betrayed she felt at my dishonesty. "I'm sorry. I want you to forgive me so we can stay friends. I don't want to lose you, Kat."

"You lost me the moment you lied to me."

"I didn't lie. What would you do if you were in my situation? Because I've gone over this in my head, like, literally a million times, and there was nothing I could've done that would've prevented all of this. I'm in this situation because of Charlie's actions, so no matter what, I'm guilty. Cut me some slack."

"Cut you some slack?" she asked incredulously. "I considered you to be my best friend, Carson. And when I say best friend, I mean the person I am most loyal to. If there's something going on behind your back, you bet your ass I'll tell you about it. You knew about all of this with Charlie, and you didn't tell me. You picked your loyalty to *him* over me. That's why I'm so upset. I was never your best friend. Otherwise, you would've betrayed him and told me."

"It wasn't like that—"

"That's exactly what it was like. You chose to keep his secret and keep me in the dark. Period."

"What would have happened if I'd told you?" I asked, having this intense conversation right on the sidewalk with other New Yorkers passing by. "It would've destroyed you. It would've made you feel worse than you already do. Why would I do that to you? I assumed Charlie would get over Denise and then forget about her. So why tell you something that you didn't really need to know? If it were me, I'd rather not know unless I absolutely had to."

She shook her head. "You aren't me. If you did tell me, I would've moved on a lot quicker, instead of waiting around, hoping we would get back together. I wasted so many months that could've been spent moving on."

I didn't have an argument against that.

"I just can't believe you sat there while I talked about Charlie all those months, and the whole time you knew he wanted to be with Denise. Are you a psychopath?"

"Of course not—"

"I just feel completely different now. I don't trust you. I'm embarrassed. I don't want anything to do with you or Charlie... or the gorgeous Denise. Just move on with your lives and forget about me. Not a single one of you ever really cared about me anyway." She turned to walk away.

"That's not true." I grabbed her by the wrist and pulled her back to me.

She twisted out of my grasp and backed away. "Don't touch me again." The threatening look in her eyes was brand-new, a look she'd never given me before, like she really hated me. "And don't bother me again either. The three of you can live happily ever after..."

When I walked in the door, Charlie stood in front of the stove in sweatpants as he cooked dinner. "We're having chicken parmesan." His bare back was to me as he stirred the sauce in the pan.

I dropped my computer bag on the table and walked away. "Cool." I went straight to my bedroom and took off my clothes and put on my pj's before I got into bed. I shut the blinds, turned off the light, and just closed my eyes.

I felt so shitty right now.

I wanted to burst into tears and cry.

My bedroom door squeaked open a few minutes later. "Everything alright?"

"I'm fine."

Footsteps didn't sound, so I knew he continued to stand there. "You don't look fine, Carson. What happened?"

"I don't want to talk about it."

He sighed loudly before he stepped farther into the room and took a seat at the edge of my bed. The mattress creaked and shifted under his weight. "Talk to me."

"I said I'm fine..." My tears were loud in my words, and that was when I realized I was crying. My lips trembled, and my eyes streamed with tears. I pulled my arms closer to my body to stop myself from shaking.

"Carson..." His hand moved to my back, and he started to rub me as he came closer. "Come on, talk to me. I've only seen you cry a couple times, so I know it's really bad."

With my face close to my bedroom wall, I continued to cry quietly, my eyes hurting as they became puffy.

"Did something happen with Dax?"

I sniffled before I gave my answer. "No."

His hand stopped moving on my back because he figured out the subject of my misery. "Kat?"

I sniffled.

He pulled his hand away altogether and sighed. "What happened?"

"I tried to talk to her after work. She said none of us ever cared about her and she wants nothing to do with me. She called me a psychopath. She doesn't want to be friends anymore." I didn't want to tell Charlie any of this to make him feel bad, but I couldn't keep it from him, not when we lived and worked together.

He went quiet like he didn't have anything to say. He continued to sit on the bed.

I took a couple deep breaths to stop myself from crying. The pain was too harsh to feel, so I did my best to pull my heart out of this darkness.

"You have no idea how sorry I am..."

I could hear the pain in his voice, feel the guilt in his energy. I knew he would do anything for me, and it was so hard, but there was nothing he could do now. "I know."

He rose off the bed and headed to the door. "I'm going to finish dinner. Do you want me to bring you a plate?"

It was the first time in my life I wasn't hungry. "No."

I LAY there and stared at the wall, the bedroom becoming darker and darker as the sun set over the city. My phone was in my bag out in the living room, so I didn't have it on me.

I didn't want to talk to anybody anyway.

The front door opened and closed, and two voices came from the living room. It was hard to make it out, but it sounded like two guys were talking. It could be Charlie and Matt, about to watch a game or something.

But then footsteps sounded down the hallway, and my bedroom door opened.

His voice was deep and affectionate, as if it pained him to see me balled up in bed like I didn't want to get up again. "Sweetheart..."

I took a deep breath when I heard his comforting voice, my eyes becoming wet again instantly.

After he undressed, he pulled back the covers and got into bed behind me. His arm circled my waist, and he pressed his chest against my back, squeezing me tight.

I turned over and faced him, let him see my wet and puffy face, let him see the heartbreak in my eyes. My arm moved around his neck, and I placed our foreheads together, feeling a little better now that he was there.

He placed a kiss to my forehead then ran his fingers through my hair. "I'm here, sweetheart. I'm right here."

11

CARSON

Hours passed, and neither one of us spoke. I didn't want to dump all my drama on him when I wanted him to make me feel better, not worse.

Just having him there made me feel better.

He spooned me from behind, his face resting against the back of my head.

Then my stomach made a loud rumble.

He inhaled a deep breath like he was trying to stop himself from laughing.

No amount of depression could eliminate my hunger.

"Do you want me to get you something to eat?"

"No. But I am hungry..."

"Charlie told me he would leave the leftovers in the fridge if we wanted any."

Now that we were talking about food, my hunger only became worse. "Let's go eat."

We got dressed and went back into the kitchen. Charlie was sitting on the couch watching the game, but he didn't say anything when we came out of my bedroom. It seemed like he wanted to give us space.

I pulled out the food from the fridge, my eyes still puffy and irritated, and put the meal in the microwave.

Dax helped himself to a bottle of water and stood with me in the kitchen as we waited for the food to warm up.

I leaned against the counter and stared at the floor.

He stared at me.

When the food was done, we sat together at the dining table, in silence.

Even when it wasn't fresh, the food was great, and I did feel a little better having something in my stomach.

Dax watched me as he ate, taking big bites as he scarfed everything down.

Charlie picked up on the energy and turned off the TV and silently excused himself to bed.

Then it was just us.

"I wish I could fix it for you."

My eyes softened at his confession, and I gave him a gentle look. "I know."

"At the end of the day, you did your best. If that's not enough for her, that's her problem, not yours. She's too emotional to see the situation pragmatically, and you would never intentionally hurt anybody."

"Thanks for trying to make me feel better, but no matter what the circumstances are, losing a friend is always painful."

"Yeah."

"Thanks for coming over."

"Anytime, sweetheart. Rain or shine, I'm here."

I didn't say anything else and continued to eat. When my plate was empty, I wiped up the sauce with my finger and licked it off.

"Are you going to try talking to her again or…give it a rest?"

I shrugged. "I'm not a quitter, but…" I also didn't waste time on lost causes. "I think it's pretty pointless. If that's how she feels, nothing I say will make her feel differently. It is what it is."

"Yeah."

"I don't want to talk about her anymore. I shed my tears and said my goodbyes…time to move on."

Dax bowed his head and looked at his plate as he considered what I'd said. It seemed like he might say something else, but he chose to stay quiet instead.

12

CHARLIE

Instead of going straight home from the office, I made a detour.

Nothing had happened between Denise and me, but she made flirty comments, stared at me a little longer than she should. So, I knew if I made a move...it would probably go somewhere. But instead of thinking about her, all I could think about was Kat.

And Carson.

Because of my idiocy, those two great people were ripped apart.

It fucking sucked.

I tried to think of something better I could have done, but there wasn't anything. I felt the way I felt—and nothing I did could change that. The only reason I didn't tell Kat was to protect her. It wasn't because I was a coward.

So I stepped off the elevator and walked down the hallway I used to take all the time. Whenever I left work, I would stop by. Sometimes I would pick her up and we would get dinner. Sometimes we would just chill in her apartment. It seemed like a lifetime ago now.

We were happy...once upon a time.

I stopped in front of her door and held my fist to the wood.

But I didn't knock.

Was this pointless?

Would this accomplish anything?

Should I just walk away and let it be?

Then I thought of Carson, the best person I'd ever known, and I let my knuckles hit the wood.

Knock. Knock. Knock.

Footsteps sounded a moment later, then a long pause, like she was standing in front of the door and looking through the peephole.

Looking at my face.

The pause continued.

Then the locks started to turn.

I inhaled a deep breath and prepared to look at her face, unsure what kind of expression would greet me.

The door opened, and she stood there, her dark hair in a braid over her shoulder, her soft eyes staring at me. The look on her face implied she hadn't expected me to show up on her doorstep ever again. A long moment of silence ensued, her looking at me...me looking at her.

I forced myself to speak up. "You got a minute?"

"Uh...sure." She stepped aside so I could enter her apartment.

Now I wondered how I hadn't noticed her feelings beforehand. We broke up and I'd just assumed she moved on, but now I could feel the energy in the room, feel her weakness for me.

I walked to the couch and turned around.

She shut the door then walked up to me, her arms crossing over her chest. She stared at the floor for a while, her eyes shifting to one foot. She was in black leggings and a loose-fitting sweater, like she intended to spend the evening in front of the TV with her favorite bottle of wine.

I had to talk again. I decided to say something gentle instead of cutting right to the chase. "How are you?"

"Um..." She cleared her throat. "Good...I guess. You?"

I felt like shit. "I'm alright."

We were back to awkward silence.

It was strange to think we were ever close at some point. We used to share every thought that came into our minds. Now she felt like a stranger because she was a different person...as was I. "I thought we should talk about everything that's been going on... It's gotten a bit crazy."

She dropped her gaze again.

I'd never actually told her how I felt about Denise to her face—and I felt sick doing it now. I tried to sidestep it. "Look, Carson isn't responsible for all of this. I was the one who made the decision. I was the one who was emotionally unfaithful. I think you should cut her some slack. There was nothing she could have done to keep everyone happy, you know? And Carson really loves you. After your last conversation, she came home and went straight to bed...and cried."

She lifted her chin when she heard those words, her eyes just a tad bit softer.

"We both know Carson. That's not like her."

Kat tucked her long hair behind her ear.

"I understand why you feel betrayed by her, but you should know that when I told her the truth, she told me that it was never going to happen, that I should forget about Denise because there would be no way to keep our friendship intact if I did otherwise. She tried to talk me out of it...a lot. But I couldn't let it go."

Now, she couldn't look at me.

"I'm so sorry, Kat. I hate that this has happened. I hated it when it was happening."

She kept a stoic face, but I knew she was crying a river inside.

"I understand if you want nothing to do with me. But

please...don't cut Carson out of your life. She really loves you, really values your friendship."

"And what about you?" She looked at me.

I stared at her for a few seconds, unsure of her meaning. "What are you asking?"

"Do you value our friendship?"

"Of course. But...I understand if that's just not an option." Seeing Denise and me together would probably be hard forever. Even if years passed, it would probably stay just as difficult to handle. "In a fantasy world, nothing would change. We can all still hang out together."

She tightened her arms across her chest and looked away, her fingers trailing along her jawline just the way she used to whenever she was deep in thought.

"Forgive Carson. Please."

"I just..." She shook her head slightly. "She lied to me."

"No." My voice grew firm. "I lied to you. I lied to you for months because I had feelings for someone else that I couldn't get under control. I wasted months of your life telling you I loved you when I didn't feel that way anymore..." It was a harsh thing to say, but I needed to direct her wrath onto me and away from Carson. "Carson has been stressed about this every single day since I first told her about it. She was angry with me because I was risking her friendship with you. You assume she was prioritizing her friendship with me, but from my perspective, yours was all she cared about."

She closed her eyes for a moment.

"Carson is the best person I know. She has the kind of integrity I haven't ever seen another person show. She's loyal to a fault. She's a good friend—the best. You know all of this because you know her as well as I do. So please, let this go."

She lifted her chin and looked at me again.

"If you're going to hate someone, hate me. I'm the reason you're hurting, not Carson."

She held my gaze for a while, the emotion glistening in her eyes. "What does she have that I don't?"

I knew we were talking about Denise now, not Carson. "Nothing."

"Then why? We were happy—"

"I know we were. And I don't know *why*. Trust me, I've asked myself that a million times." My hands ran up my face and into my hair so I could grip the strands. "I tried to brush it off, but that only made it worse. It doesn't make sense. I don't have an answer for you. But it's not you. You've never been the problem. It's not because you aren't pretty enough or interesting enough. It's not you."

She dropped her chin again like she couldn't meet my look. "Is it because she's Carson's sister?"

"Meaning?"

She looked at me again. "You're so close with Carson. Maybe this is a way to be with Carson without actually being with her."

My eyes narrowed at the accusation. "I don't have feelings for Carson. That's ridiculous. If that were the case, I would have done something about it by now. There's zero attraction there. I've seen her naked and, still, nothing. And trust me, I'm straight."

"That's why it makes even more sense."

My eyes narrowed in confusion.

"You love Carson, but you aren't attracted to her. Denise is a version of her that you're attracted to."

"Denise and Carson are nothing alike."

"Well, that's the only explanation I can think of—and it makes sense."

I'd never examined my own actions before, but I didn't think that was the case. Or maybe it was, because I'd never felt this way about anyone before. If Denise and I ended up together, Carson and I would be related, and she would always be in my life, which was nice. My children would be related to her.

"At least that's what I tell myself to make me feel better. That I didn't have a chance."

That part was true, based on the potency of my feelings. "The reason doesn't matter. What does matter is your friendship with Carson. Don't lose something so great because I'm a jackass. Good friends are hard to come by."

"I know that."

"Then...forgive her."

"I'm still angry right now—"

"Then take some time, but don't throw it away. We both know you're never going to find a friend as good as Carson. You can't afford to lose her, frankly. This city is huge, but it can be the loneliest place in the world."

She looked into my eyes awhile, her thoughts a mystery.

"I'd really like it if we could be friends too...someday."

She tucked her hair behind her again, even though it was already placed there. It was an absent-minded action she'd always made.

"But I understand if we can't. I'm just putting that out there."

She nodded. "I appreciate you saying that." When it was just her and me like this, she was vulnerable and small, like she wanted to move into a corner and disappear. My proximity affected her, made her nervous and excited at the same time. "Kat...you're beautiful."

She lifted her gaze and looked at me, grabbing on to those words like a lifeline.

"Some guy is going to come along, and he won't be able to believe that he found you. He'll worship the ground you walk on, love you in a way I never did. You'll be the love of his life. I'm sorry it wasn't me, but whoever replaces me will be much better."

"Maybe..." Her voice cracked when her suppressed

emotion shone through. "But honestly...you're the love of my life."

A wrecking ball just crashed into my chest—and I couldn't react. I couldn't show my pity, couldn't show my self-loathing. "That will change. I promise. When you meet the perfect person, I'll mean nothing to you. You'll wonder why you ever felt anything for me at all, because I'm kind of a douchebag."

Her wet eyes suddenly calmed as a laugh escaped her lips.

A smile broke across my lips when I heard that sound. "I am. We both know it."

After she chuckled for a bit, her eyes started to dry. "No, you aren't."

"I'm pretty sure Carson would disagree with you."

"And she would be teasing if she did."

I looked at Kat and felt the atmosphere change, felt the energy become less hostile. The ice around her heart had been broken, and the kind person I knew shone through. "Think about what I said, okay? We all love you very much."

"Including you?"

My eyes softened. "If you ever really loved someone, you never stop. And if you don't love them, you never did in the first place. You know which one applies to us."

When I came home, Carson's laptop was open on the dining table, but she was sprawled out on the couch, her feet on the edge of the armrest, a blanket pulled over her with a margarita on the coffee table.

Normally, I would talk some shit right now, but she was obviously hurting. "What are you watching?"

"You know..." She spoke in a bored voice like she didn't even care what was on the screen. "Keeping Up with the Bitches...whatever it's called."

Carson rarely watched TV unless it was sports or the news. "And why are you watching that?"

"Because I wish I were a rich bitch, walking around, stirring up shit…"

I set my bag on the counter and sighed because Carson had really fallen into the rabbit hole. "I need to talk to you."

She crossed her ankles on the edge of the couch, her slippers visible. "Go ahead. Talk."

I entered the living room and got a full view of her, in her pajamas with her hair in a ponytail. There was a chocolate stain on the front of her shirt, and she hadn't worn makeup to the office, even though she always did. "I talked to Kat today. I saw her right before I came home, actually."

She stilled at my words before she quickly sat up. "Seriously? What happened? What did you say? What did she say?" All the questions rolled out of her mouth at the same time, so it was just a jumbled mess.

"Chill out, and I'll tell you."

Her ponytail was high in the center of her head, and the hair shifted in front of her face, so she had to fling it away.

"I basically told her you've been really sad about the whole thing…and she should forgive you. I told her I was the one who made the decision and you've been rooting for her the entire time, which is true."

"And…?" She took a deep breath like my answer was a lifeline.

"She said she would think about it."

Disappointment filled her gaze.

"I think she'll come around. She just needs some time. I told her I'd like it if we could all be friends, so we'll see how she responds."

She nodded before she took another deep breath. "Well… thanks for doing that."

"I won't let you lose her because of me. That's not right."

She shrugged. "Sometimes, that's how life works out."

"Well, that's not how this is going to work out. I'll make this right...eventually."

"God, I hope so. I've felt like shit like every single moment of every day."

"Yeah...I noticed." I grabbed the remote and changed the channel. "And turn this shit off. You're better than this."

"Better than rich-bitch drama?" she asked. "No one is better than that. But I know the game is on, so I'll let you change it." She already seemed better, a slight smile moving onto her lips. Her eyes were a little lighter, and the old Carson started to come back into view. Then she asked the question that told me everything would be okay. "So, what's for dinner?"

13

DAX

"I'm so happy to hear that." I sat across from Charlie in the bar, waiting for Carson to show up. "It's really been eating away at her, and it kills me to see her like that."

"Me too." His hand rested on the top of his glass, his eyes down. "So, hopefully, Kat comes around. I felt like it was a good conversation. I mean...it went better than I thought it would."

"I'm sure she will. Not to seem insensitive, but I think she's being unfair, blaming Carson for everything."

"That makes two of us," he said quickly. "But she's just emotional and hurt, not thinking clearly, and she's stubborn. So, I'm afraid that stubbornness will last a long time, until the point when it's too late."

I nodded in agreement. "You're probably right."

He brought his beer to his lips and took a drink. "Carson's been turning to you for comfort, though...that must be nice."

I didn't want Carson to be upset about everything, but I couldn't lie about that. It was nice to be the first person she went to instead of Charlie. "It is."

"And it's nice for me because I have so much more free time on my hands," he said with a chuckle.

"And what are you doing with this free time?"

He lowered his beer to the table and shrugged. "Nothing, actually."

"And is that going to change?" This guy had the willpower to hold off for a long time, so how did he still have the strength to keep up that restraint?

He shrugged. "You think I should?"

"Only your dick can answer that question."

He released another chuckle. "He and I never agree on anything."

"Anything?" I asked incredulously. "I find that hard to believe."

He grinned. "I guess I wanted to wait until Kat and Carson officially made up, but I have no idea when that will be."

Now I understood why he and Carson were so close. They were both so selfless, always putting everyone else's needs before their own. "Who knows when that will be or if it will even happen? You deserve to be happy, Charlie. Go for it."

"You think so?"

"Yeah, man. It's been a long time…"

He stared at his beer for a while before he gave a nod. "Yeah, it has." He brought his beer to his lips and took a drink before he looked across the bar, clearly thinking of something else. "Yeah…I think I will."

"Good. When are you going to go for it?"

He shrugged. "Next time I see her…maybe."

"Good luck. But I have a feeling you don't need it."

He turned back to me, a slight smile on his lips. "I think she's into me, which has made this so much harder. But I guess the wait is over. I haven't been seeing anyone for a while now, so that's made it even more challenging."

"That's sweet, Charlie."

"Or lame, depending on how you look at it."

"If someone means something to you, the wait is always

worth it." Carson popped into my mind, the woman who was so much more than sex, so much more than all the superficial sensations of lust. I waited a long time for her, but I would have waited longer.

"Okay, now you're lame," he teased.

I shrugged in guilt. "Yeah, I've been pretty lame since I settled down." I'd closed the doors on my playboy lifestyle and turned into a monogamous and committed man—and it wasn't hard. I didn't miss my past at all. It was just money and loneliness. The reason I wanted Carson to meet my rich friends was for them to understand why I declined their invitations to party. Instead of giving me shit about it, they would see she was a great woman and respect that.

"Are you going to ask her to move in?"

I stared at him for a while, surprised by the question. "Why do you ask?"

"Because it'll be nice to get my apartment back. When I walked into the apartment the other day, she was watching some stupid reality show on the couch with dishes in the sink and shit everywhere. Be nice to have the place to myself again."

I took a drink to suppress my grin. "You're really selling it, man."

He laughed. "That was a stupid thing to say, huh? I mean, she's not all that bad…" He took a drink of his beer.

Even if she was a slob, it wouldn't bother me. I was sure she would be different living with me, because we were partners rather than roommates.

"And I just want some privacy for Denise. I bring girls to the apartment all the time, but none of them have ever been her sister. So that's a little weird. I hear you guys going at it sometimes, and I know she hears me, so…"

"Yeah, that would be weird."

"So, I need you to take her off my hands."

I chucked. "Your suggestion has been received."

"You know I'm kidding, right?" He looked at me over the top of his glass. "No pressure."

I loved having her over, loved fucking her first thing in the morning before I was even fully awake. We made dinner together in the kitchen as an evening ritual, and sometimes we watched a game on TV before we got nasty on the couch. I loved having her around. I wished I had her around more. "Yeah, I know."

His eyes moved to the TV as he continued to enjoy his beer, his blond hair getting a little long, like he needed a haircut. He leaned back against the booth and rested his arm over the top, his eyes still on the TV, sitting with me like I was Matt instead of the man seeing his best friend. It seemed like we were actually friends, not just acquaintances.

"Can I ask you something?"

His eyes shifted back to me. "Go for it."

"This stays between us, alright?"

"Oh shit…" He dropped his arm from the back of the booth. "That doesn't sound good."

"Should I worry about Carson? You know, with her job."

Charlie stared at me in silence, a deer in the headlights.

"She ran into one of the guys she's trying to lock up at the charity event last weekend, and I know she brushes off stuff like this and makes it a joke…but she seemed different, even days afterward. And there was one night she was tailing some guy at a club I was at, and he was about to punch her in the alleyway, but thankfully I was there."

He was stone-faced.

"Never mind…I have my answer." I'd hoped Charlie would tell me something to make me feel better, like they had the best security to look after them, but I knew that wasn't true. Carson's job was just as dangerous as I'd assumed it was.

He continued to stare at me, helpless to say something to make me feel better.

"What would happen if I asked her to stop?"

"As in...quit her job?"

I nodded. "Not necessarily quit. Just move into a different department. Do something less dangerous."

He gave a long and drawn-out sigh. "Unlikely. She worked really hard to move up the ranks and get this position. There're not a lot of women who have been promoted this high, and if she steps out, she'll see it as an insult to all women."

"It's not insulting. It's not even about gender. It's dangerous to anyone who does it."

"Yeah, I know."

"What about you?"

"What about me?" he asked.

"Are you in the same boat?"

"No," he answered. "I have some high-profile articles, but not at her caliber."

"And if you could, would you do it?"

"Uh..." He gave a long shrug. "I really don't know. I'm almost thirty, and I'm hoping to settle down so...maybe not."

Charlie thought this way, so why couldn't Carson?

"I always remind her that the article is never worth her life. That nothing is worth her life. But you know how she is..."

Fearless.

"I don't think you'd accomplish anything by asking her to step down. It would probably just put distance between you. So, you're just going to have to accept it if you want to be with her. I know that's hard, but..."

I couldn't accept that. "I don't care if she's a workaholic who cares more about her job than anything else. I just want her to be safe. Why can't she work at *Runway* like in *The Devil Wears Prada* or something?"

His elbows moved to the table as he chuckled. "Wow, I could not picture Carson doing that."

Me neither.

"You guys are finally together, so I would just leave it alone."

"We're together—for now." I rubbed my jawline as I sighed. "But I don't want to be together just for now. I want to be together forever. I told her I want her to be my wife, to have a couple kids with her. How is that possible when she's out there risking her neck, going head to head with corporate criminals? When she's hanging out with the mob?"

"Yeah. I get it." He gave a slight nod. "In life, things change, priorities change. Maybe in time she'll feel differently as your commitment changes. I know she's stubborn, but she's also realistic. And I know how much she loves you, so if it gets to that level, I'm sure she'll reevaluate. Who would pick a job over the love of your life, you know?"

"Well…I feel like our commitment is already changing."

"Yeah?" He set down his beer and examined my expression. "As in…you do want to ask her to move in?"

When we met, I wasn't even ready for a serious relationship, which was obvious by all the lies I told. Having a fake apartment for my hookups was pretty indicative of my mental state. But once the truth was out, everything was different. She was the one thing I wanted more than anything, and my money didn't mean anything to her. I wasn't worried about the past repeating itself. All I wanted was to be happy, and she made me really happy. I wasn't ready—and now I was ready for it all. "Yeah. I do."

14

CARSON

I LEFT THE BUILDING WITH A FOLDER OF PAPERWORK slipped into my computer bag. I had a source that was able to give me all the documentation to outline the money trail, to find out who their manufacturers were. All I'd have to do was get a couple guys on record, and I'd have the smoking gun.

My phone vibrated in my pocket.

I immediately answered it in my typical reporter fashion. "Carson."

His smile was audible in his tone. "Dax."

"Oh hey," I said excitedly. "Sorry, I just finished up with an appointment, and I'm in my crazy journalist mode."

There was a long pause, almost like he hadn't heard what I said. Then he ignored it altogether. "Wanted to see if you wanted to get dinner. I just left the office."

"I am hungry...but what's new?"

He chuckled. "What are you in the mood for?"

"Maybe a burger or something. Is that cool?"

"Sure."

"Have you been to Mega Shake?"

"Mega what?" he asked, chuckling slightly.

"They've got these greasy-ass burgers and these super

creamy milk shakes. How do you not know it? You've lived in Manhattan your entire life."

"I guess I didn't hang out with the cool kids. I'll meet you there."

"Alright. See you soon." I hung up and walked quicker because I was a few blocks away, and I was starving. Minutes later, I walked inside the joint and spotted Dax sitting in one of the booths in his ultra-expensive suit. He looked totally out of place—but still sexy.

He slid his phone into his pocket and rose to greet me, having that sexy shadow along his jawline. He smiled slightly, but his eyes shone much brighter than his mouth, like seeing me was the highlight of his long day. "Hey, sweetheart." His arm circled my waist, and he leaned down to kiss me.

I melted at his touch, loving the affection in his lips, loving the way he loved me without even saying it.

He pulled away but kept his arm around my waist. "What's good here?"

"Step aside. I got this." I walked up to the register, ordered food for both of us, and then handed over my card.

Dax didn't try to pay for everything all the time. He respected my desire for equality—and that was nice. He never made a stink about his being a billionaire and that the cost of food was literally cents on the dollar to him.

We sat in the booth together with our sodas and listened to the cooks fry everything up.

My computer bag was on the seat beside me against the window, and my ass sighed in relief now that I got to sit down. I'd been running around all day. "How was your day?"

"You know...meetings." His elbows rested on the table, his wrists slightly exposed along with his Omega watch. His brown hair was perfectly styled like he was ready for a public appearance on the *Today Show*. "It's much better now."

I smiled. "I'm glad I'm more exciting than running a Fortune 500 company."

"Not too many women can say that."

I smiled again. "I'm not sure if I deserve that, but thank you."

"Oh, you definitely do. So, how was your day?"

"Busy. I ran around everywhere." I pulled my bag close to me and patted it with my hand. "But I got all the paperwork I need from a source to do some digging. I've got their manufacturers, so I'll do a few interviews on the record. Pretty potent evidence."

He gave me a blank look before he nodded. "Sounds like you're making progress."

"I'm doing double time. Gotta stay ten steps ahead."

Now, the energy at the table was totally different. His affection was long gone, his eyes no longer soft and glued to my face. He turned away and stared across the restaurant, at nothing, really.

I glanced at the cooks and saw them creating our trays of food. I turned back to Dax, who still wasn't looking at me.

The guy brought the trays over then walked away.

I grabbed a couple fries and put them into my mouth.

He didn't touch his food. Instead, he stared at it like he'd lost his appetite.

"Did I say something?" He'd taken the sunshine away, and now I was freezing cold.

He stared down for a long time before he grabbed the edge of his tray and pushed it to the side.

When he did that, I lost my appetite too.

"I'm just going to be candid with you right now." His hands came together on the surface like he was in a meeting and I was a difficult client. "Because I don't know how else to handle this, and you seem to respond to bluntness."

"Okay…" We were happy, like, two seconds ago, and now it was tense.

"I want to ask you to marry me." He stared at me with that hard look, his statement aggressive rather than romantic.

I stopped breathing because I couldn't believe what he'd said, right in the middle of Mega Shake.

"But I can't do that if your professional focus continues. I want to do whatever is necessary to make you happy, but I'll never be happy knowing you're sticking your neck out like this every single day, that you've got a target on your back everywhere you go, that you're in the top ten most dangerous professions in the world. I just can't."

I didn't expect him to dump that on me like this.

"Charlie told me to keep my mouth shut and just be happy right now, but I can't. Because I want to be happy forever, not just now. When I said I wanted you to be my wife, I meant it. This isn't just a relationship to me. I can't have my wife putting herself in danger, not when I love her more than anything. And I want kids with you. We haven't talked about this and I know it's premature, but I really want that. So..."

I dropped my gaze, my heart beating so hard. "You're dumping me..."

"No." His quiet voice had a hurt tone.

I looked at him again.

"I'm telling you that I want to marry you, and if I ask... would you be willing to make this compromise? I don't care if you're a workaholic and you want to remain devoted to a career. I can take a step back at work and take care of the kids so you can pursue your dream. That's not a problem. I will support whatever you want to do, and we'll make it work. But...it can't be dangerous like this. There are lots of other respectable kinds of journalism you can do that aren't dangerous. Is this something you're willing to do...to be with me?"

He'd unloaded the heaviest question I'd ever been asked. Normally, my answer would be an instinctual no, and I would walk out of there without looking back. But I really loved this man, and I didn't want to lose the greatest thing that had ever happened to me.

He waited for me to give him an answer, his features tight like he anticipated I would say no.

"Can I think about it...?"

His eyebrows immediately rose, as if he couldn't believe what I'd just said. His hands tightened together on the table as he tensed. "Yes. Take all the time you need."

We sat there together and stared at each other, the sound of the cooks in the background, our food getting cold on the table.

His watch clanked against the table when he moved his wrist. "I expected you to just say no."

"That sounds like an answer I would give."

His eyes turned soft again, the affection returning. "Just the fact that you're willing to think about it...means a lot to me."

CHARLIE STOOD at the kitchen counter, the hot pan sizzling as he prepared dinner. He must have heard me walk inside because he said, "Chicken kebabs."

"Already ate." I dropped my bag on the table and pulled out the paperwork I had secured that afternoon.

"What did you have?" He turned around to look at me.

"Mega Shake."

"And you didn't bring me anything?"

"I know you don't eat shit all the time like I do, so I assumed you would pass." I took a seat and pulled out my laptop so I could get back to work. Whenever I was down, that was what I usually did, threw myself into work.

Charlie stared at me for another minute before he turned back to the stove and finished cooking.

I looked through the paperwork and made my notes.

Charlie carried his dinner to the spot across from me and took a seat. "You seem down."

"Just a little…overwhelmed." Dax had just dropped a ton of bricks on my shoulders, and I hadn't recovered from the event.

He glanced at my paperwork as he took a bite and chewed. "I told you to hand it back to Vince if it was too much for you—"

"That's not the problem." I set my paperwork down and looked at him. "Dax told me he wanted to ask me to marry him."

His mouth was full of food, but he stopped chewing, his cheeks full. It seemed to be too much effort to chew it and swallow it quickly, so he just spat it out into a napkin so he could respond fast. "*What?*"

"But he said he didn't think he could…if I continue this line of work."

Charlie ignored his dinner altogether and let it get cold because this conversation was more important than a hot meal.

"He said he just worries about me, and he doesn't want to worry about his wife all the time, for his kids to worry about their mother all the time."

"Jesus, he came on strong, didn't he?"

I shrugged. "A bit."

"So…" He looked at me as if he expected me to finish his sentence. "What does that mean? Did you guys break up?"

I shook my head. "No. I just said I needed to think about it. He basically gave me an ultimatum. He can't be married to a woman who's always in danger. He loves me too much to suffer through it. I get it."

With his arms on the table, he stared at me.

"So if he asked me to marry him and I say yes…that means I agree to move into another discipline of journalism."

He looked at me with new eyes. "I can't believe you would even consider it."

My eyes narrowed on his face.

"Not in a bad way. That's just not something you would normally do, which means you really love this guy."

I gave a nod. "I do."

"Wow..." He sank back into his chair and rubbed the back of his head.

"There were a couple other things he said that changed my attitude about it. For one, he said he didn't mind if I wanted to be a workaholic for the rest of my life. He would take a step back at work and be the caretaker for our children. How many men would say something like that?"

He shrugged. "Not many."

"And he said he would be supportive of my career, no matter what, that we would make it work. He's never asked me to stop working because he's a billionaire who can support me. He gets me. He understands that my career is important to me."

"Yeah, he's a good guy."

"So, can I really throw that away for a job? Because a guy like Dax isn't going to come around again."

He shook his head. "You're right. He's one of a kind."

I didn't immediately explode with my feminist verbiage when he'd asked me to make a compromise because he'd offered to make compromises too. He agreed to be the primary parent so I could chase my dream, and being a full-time dad was not something most men fantasized about. And his requests didn't stem from his need to control me or make me do what he wanted. He just wanted to keep me safe, and I couldn't lie and say my job wasn't dangerous. It could be really fucking dangerous. "I think I'm going to tell him yes."

Charlie looked at me with brand-new eyes, as if he saw me as a whole new person. "I think that's the right answer."

My job was important to me, but my professional track record had already established my credibility and commitment. Life wouldn't always stay the same. It changed, and you had to change with it. Now, I had a man who had become part of my family, and it would be really stupid to risk losing that for a job. Yes, it was important to me, but at the end of the day, it was just a job.

He was worth a lot more than that.

Charlie smiled. "Ready to go back to the Lifestyle section?"

I rolled my eyes and released a loud sigh. "I'll die before I do that."

He chuckled. "You've had a great career at the *New York Press,* so I'm sure you can get a job at any other magazine or news outlet that you want. Dax even told me he wishes you would work for a fashion magazine like in *The Devil Wears Prada.*"

I rolled my eyes. "I couldn't write about shoes all day. I could *buy* shoes all day, sure. But I don't have much to say about them."

"I'm really proud of you. Instead of shutting everything out, you're letting things in, you're being human again. It's really nice to see."

I knew I had changed so much, that the moment Dax walked into my life, I started to heal from the past. Without him, I wasn't sure if I ever would've made it to this place. "Yeah... It is."

15

DAX

I couldn't believe she'd said she'd think about it.

This was Carson we were talking about.

She didn't give up territory for anything.

But she actually considered it...for me.

It made me feel just as good as if she'd said yes. It made me feel important to her, that I was just as significant in her life as her friends. I'd moved into the inner circle, becoming more than just a boyfriend to her, but family.

That was the greatest compliment I'd ever received.

A week passed, and I didn't bring it up to her. She came over to my place some nights, and the others, I went over to hers. We talked about anything but the one thing we were both thinking about. That was okay with me.

I got to the gym with the guys, and we warmed up with a couple shots, running around with our shirts off and working up a sweat. When Carson walked in with her friends, I immediately abandoned the court and walked over to them.

Charlie sat on the bleachers with Denise beside him, the two of them engaged in conversation. Matt sat a short distance away, as if he were giving them space so his friend could seal the deal. Carson was beside him, and when I walked over, she rose to her feet.

I smiled at her cuteness, loving her little workout shorts and her t-shirt. I liked it when her hair was pulled back so I could see more of her beautiful face. "Hey, sweetheart—"

"Yes." She stood with her hands on her hips, giving me a serious look, her eyes focused on my face like this was a business deal rather than a personal conversation between two people in love.

My smile faded when I heard that single word, the unexpected answer to a conversation we'd had over a week ago. I inhaled a deep breath when I heard that answer, the trumpets playing in my ears. I stood in front of her, looking down at her without touching her.

Her eyes shifted back and forth as she gazed into my face.

I couldn't speak. Couldn't think. All I could do was absorb that answer further into my bloodstream, memorize her tone as she spat it out in the middle of a basketball court at a gym. It was blunt and to the point—exactly who she was.

She walked past me then headed onto the court as she joined the guys for a warm-up.

I watched her go before I turned back to her friends.

Charlie gave a slight shrug. "I couldn't believe it either."

AFTER THE GAME, we got pizza and wings, as was tradition. The food was so heavy and greasy that it seemed to negate all the exercise we'd just done on the court. I sat beside Carson as we drank our beers and waited for the food to come out.

Charlie was absorbed in Denise, making her laugh and smile, like they were already a couple that hadn't actually touched each other.

My hand went to Carson's bare thigh under the table.

She turned to me once she felt my affection.

I gave her a gentle squeeze as I looked down at her, finding her to be the most beautiful woman in the world even when her skin was shiny with sweat and she didn't wear makeup. "I love you."

Her eyes softened. "I love you too."

I wanted to talk about her answer from before, but I almost felt like it was better left unsaid. She'd abandoned all her old ways and completely let me in. It was the biggest declaration of love she could ever make. "So...you want to have kids?" I'd never actually asked her before. I just inserted her into my dream, pictured her as the mother of my children.

She shrugged. "Someday...maybe. I'm open-minded about it."

"I think you'd be a great mom."

"I don't know about that." She shrugged off my compliment. "I'd probably be a drill sergeant."

"And is that a bad thing?"

"Well, I'd have to be the disciplinarian since you'll be the teddy bear."

I shrugged. "I'm an excellent cuddle buddy."

She smiled. "You are."

The waitress brought all the food and placed it on the table.

Matt clapped his hands. "Alright. Let's do this."

Charlie didn't seem to notice the food because he was so absorbed in his conversation with Denise.

Carson immediately grabbed some wings and fries.

I let her go first—as always. "You think he's going for it?"

She glanced at them across the table, visibly smitten with each other. "I hope so. About time he put his money where his mouth is."

"You think he'll tell her he's felt this way for a long time?"

"I hope not. Kinda creepy."

"Creepy?" I asked.

"Could you imagine telling someone you've been obsessed

with them for, like, a year? That you dumped your last partner because you couldn't stop thinking about them?" She put a few fries into her mouth. "I think it's a little much."

"Yeah, I guess."

"He can tell her…but just wait a while."

I put the food on my plate. "Have you talked to her about everything?"

She shook her head. "I do my best to stay out of things. Learned my lesson."

"There was no lesson to learn because it wasn't your fault."

She shrugged. "Not everyone shares that opinion."

My hand moved to her back, and I gently rubbed her before massaging the back of her neck. "But they will, in time."

She lay beside me in the dark, surrounded by windows that showed the city glow outside. The sheets were pulled to her shoulder and covered her naked body, and her hair was all over the place from the way I'd fisted it. She released a loud sigh, as if it was an announcement. "I should probably go. I have to get up early tomorrow…"

"Why don't you just bring a bag?" I lay beside her and stared at her.

"Because I'm lazy. I hate packing."

"Then why don't you bring some things to keep here? A couple outfits? Extra makeup?"

"So, you can have girlie shit in your closet and on your bathroom counter?" she asked incredulously.

"I don't mind. It just reminds me that you'll come back."

Her lips relaxed slightly at my words. "You know I'll always come back, even if I don't have anything here."

"I do."

She sat up and looked at the clock on my nightstand.

"Why do you have to get up early?"

"Staff meeting."

"Oh, I know how that goes."

"I have to give details about everything I'm working on, just like everyone else in the office does. It's kind of annoying because no one really cares what anyone else is doing because we're so focused on our own articles, but I get why it saves my editor time."

"You know, my place is closer to your office, so you're actually closer when you stay here."

She grinned at my attempt to keep her around. "Which makes it an even farther commute when I have to go back to my apartment first."

"Which is why you need to keep stuff here. Besides, don't you want to be out of the apartment when Denise and Charlie start sleeping together?"

She cringed. "Very true...and well played."

I propped myself on my arm and moved my hand into her hair so I could kiss her, taste the lips I'd already tasted all night. "Come on, sweetheart. Ditch that place and come live with me."

Her eyes shifted back and forth as she looked into my face. "It sounds like you're asking me to move in with you."

"If your answer is yes, I am. If it's not...you're reading too much into it."

She continued to study me, her face unreadable. "You think this is going too fast?"

We'd just hit a roadblock, and the collision was painful. "Do you?"

"No... Isn't that weird?"

My eyes immediately narrowed on her face because I couldn't believe what she'd said. "It's not weird at all." It wasn't weird because it felt right—for both of us. "I think we've gotten exactly what we deserve in each other. And that's not weird."

Her eyes filled with affection as she smiled.

"Could you imagine doing this every day? Every night?"

"I can. But I think after you talk to Charlie, he'll convince you it's a bad idea. He'll tell you about the popcorn in the couch cushions, the time I used his phone as a flashlight and dropped it in the toilet, and how I vacuumed the entire apartment when the bag was full, so I ended up making the entire place even dirtier."

"He might have mentioned a couple things."

"Well, there you go."

"But I also think he wants to get you out of that apartment as fast as possible."

"That's what he says, but…I don't know." Her smile faded, and she turned more serious. "We've been living together for a long time. I think he'd actually be pretty sad if I left. I'd be kind of sad too, you know."

"Yeah, I understand," I said gently.

"But I also understand that people move on, and that's not a bad thing."

Her living with me definitely wasn't a bad thing.

"So, if my answer was yes…where would we live?"

"Here."

"In a penthouse?" she asked, slightly incredulous.

"Is that a problem?"

"I don't know…" She took a look around at all the luxury. "Not really my thing. You know I'm a burger and fries kind of girl. I'm not into Cristal and caviar. I keep it real."

"Is there somewhere else you'd like to live?"

Her eyes narrowed slightly. "I get the option?"

"Of course. I want to be with you—even if that means renting the apartment above Mega Shake."

When she laughed, it was so beautiful, the smile that stretched across her face. Her eyes lit up like fireworks, and I memorized it so I could think about it during my boring meetings, when I had to work late and couldn't be with her. "I don't know if I'd want to live there…"

"Then wherever you want. I really don't care."

Her hand moved to my arm, and she gently rubbed my skin, her gaze becoming serious. "Here is fine."

"You're sure?"

She nodded. "Moving is a bitch."

My lips softened into a smile. "It sounds like you're saying yes..."

Her cheeks started to blush slightly, like she couldn't believe she was making such a spontaneous decision. "Well, are you saying yes?"

"Yes. A million times."

"Then...yes."

I inhaled a deep breath as I looked at the confidence in her gaze, the fact that she knew she wanted to be with me, to leave the comfort of her home and start a life with me. It was like living in a dream, having the one woman you wanted want you in the same way. "That makes me really happy."

"It does?" she whispered.

"Yes. Just don't try to vacuum."

That laughter came back, reaching her eyes. Her laughter was infectious, so I joined her.

"Alright...I guess I'm moving. But I could just leave my stuff there, and Charlie can turn my room into a guest bedroom."

"You're welcome to bring your stuff here. I can get rid of some things to make room."

Her eyes softened all over again, reaching a new depth.

"What?" I whispered.

"That was why I said yes."

I stared at her face, unsure what she meant. But I knew she would tell me if I gave her the floor.

"That's why I agreed to compromise. Because you're willing to compromise. When you told me you would step down as the big CEO to be there for our kids so I could keep working, that meant a lot to me. To find a man who would step back so I could go first...is impossible to describe. You're a billionaire, but you'll never make a fuss about me staying home and doing yoga or some shit. You'll let me live my life the way I want so I'll have no regrets. And if any woman is lucky enough to find a man like that, she's got to do whatever she can to hold on to him."

Transfixed by the emotion in her face, I stared at her. "Because I'm the right man for you...just as you're the right woman for me."

16

CARSON

Charlie sat on the couch and watched the TV, a beer on the table beside him. He was in sweatpants and a shirt, watching the TV with a sleepy gaze like he was ready for bed but too lazy to get up and walk into the bedroom.

"So, what's going on with Denise?"

Charlie turned to look at me, clearly surprised by the question. "Nothing. We're just talking."

"Why is that all you're doing?"

He shrugged. "I don't know. Still seems weird."

"I think it's weirder that you haven't done anything."

He gave another shrug. "I guess."

"And I'm moving out, so...you should think about who will replace me."

Charlie did a double take when he heard that information. "Say what? Back up. You're moving out? And where are you going?"

"Oh, come on. Where do you think I'm going?" I rolled my eyes.

"He asked you to move in with him?"

I nodded. "Yep."

"Wow…Carson is moving out." He threw his arms in the air in celebration. "Fuck yes."

I rolled my eyes again. "Whatever. I know you're sad."

"I'm not sad at all."

"Yes, you are."

He pivoted his body to look at me straight on. "On a scale of one to ten, my sadness level is a one." He held up a single finger.

"Bullshit. It's a seven."

"Maybe a two."

"Six." I felt like we were negotiating back and forth over a deal.

His eyes narrowed. "Four."

"Five."

He paused for a while before he gave a slight nod. "Okay…five."

I smiled. "I knew it."

"So I'm half-and-half. I'm happy that you are moving in with this guy and getting on with your life, but I'm also sad that I won't get to see you all the time."

"What about work?"

"You won't be doing that for long either, right?"

"He asked me to move in with him. Not marry him."

"But that's next on the list."

It would be weird not to see Charlie every single day, for him not to be the person I spoke to the most. But Dax had already replaced him in a lot of ways. I hadn't really noticed until now.

"We'll still see each other all the time. Whether Denise and I get together or not. That's a promise."

"I know. But I do hope you and Denise get together—and get married and have a bunch of babies."

He chuckled. "For now, I just want us to get together."

"You want me to talk to her?"

He shook his head. "I can talk to a woman on my own."

"I mean about Kat."

"You haven't told her what happened?"

I shook my head. "I didn't think I could really talk to her about anything, so she has no idea."

"And that also means Denise hasn't mentioned me to you either."

"I try to stay out of your relationship as much as possible, learn from my mistakes."

He gave me a sad look. "Maybe you should tell her about Kat, that way she knows it's okay to say yes when I go for it."

"What happened to you not needing me to talk to a woman for you?" I teased.

"I just think having to have a conversation after I make my move will interfere with all the making out we might do."

I made a disgusted face. "Gross."

"Get used to it. I have to watch Dax grab your ass all the time and make out with you in between hot wings, so..."

"But he's not your brother."

"But you're like my sister."

I shook my head and looked at the TV. "I guess I'll get used to it."

"So, when are you moving in with Dax?"

I shrugged. "No specific date. It's pretty casual."

"And you're okay living in a big-ass penthouse?"

"He said he was willing to get an apartment with me, but I thought it would be stupid for him to move out just on principle. He's got a lot of money, and if I want to spend my life with him, I'll just have to get used to it."

He nodded in agreement. "Very true. Isn't it weird to think that when you get married, you'll be a billionaire too?"

I didn't think I'd ever get used to that. I'd probably have my own bank account and my own money, but just live in his house. "I know when people get married, they share their finances, but I just can't see myself doing that. I'll live in whatever house he wants to buy, but I'll never consider his money as my money."

"Why do you have such a hard time accepting his wealth? I know money isn't important to you, but you seem to despise it."

I turned back to him. "Because I've written a lot of articles about rich people. It's very rare to hear a story that has a happy ending. The money makes them greedy and evil, and the wealth ends up destroying their lives instead of making it better. Money is the root of all evil, in my opinion. So, I honestly want nothing to do with it."

He nodded in understanding. "Yeah, that makes sense. But with Dax, it seems like his story will have a happy ending."

I couldn't agree more. That was why I was willing to do all of this to be with him. "I think so too."

"You're really moving in with him?" Denise asked me from across the table in the sushi restaurant, holding her chopsticks between her fingers. "You? Carson?"

"Yep. The rumors are true."

She grabbed a sushi roll and placed it in her mouth. After a couple bites, she shook her head again. "I'm really happy for you. Just surprised."

"Trust me, I was really surprised too. Not surprised that he asked, surprised that I wanted the same things."

"For what it's worth, he's so much better than Evan ever was. You can tell he's genuinely a good guy. Not to mention, he's super hot."

"Yeah. Another reason why I said yes." I chuckled before I took a bite of my roll. "Do you know who else is super hot? Charlie."

Her eyebrows rose up on her face. "What did you just

say?" She turned jealous immediately, just the way I did about Dax.

Her reaction told me everything I needed to know. "Girl, he's all yours. Not my type. But maybe you should go for him..."

Her wrath slowly subsided. "Do I make it that obvious?"

"You both do. I think it's time for something to happen."

"I don't know... I really don't want to hurt Kat." She bowed her head and pushed her rolls around with her chopsticks.

"I think it's time for all of us to move on. And you and Charlie would be great together, so I think you guys should give it a go."

"Really?" she asked in surprise.

"Yeah. Charlie talked to her recently and told her that he wanted to ask you out."

"Shut up! He did not."

"Yep. She wasn't thrilled about it, but he said it seemed like she understood."

"Oh my god. She must hate me."

"No. She and I aren't on good terms...but you guys are fine."

"Wait, what happened with you?" my sister asked.

I'd never told her about it because I had no explanation. I couldn't just tell her that I knew Charlie had been hung up on her this long. It would make him look like a weirdo. "I told her that she needed to move on with her life and not stand in the way of you and Charlie wanting to get together. She didn't like that, so we haven't really been talking. I think she just needs some time."

"Whoa... I don't know what to say."

"It was for her own good. Because she still has feelings for him, and he doesn't feel the same way at all. I think it was a kick in the chest but what she needed to hear."

She set her chopsticks on her plate and stared down at her food like she didn't know what to do.

"Damage is done, Denise. You guys should just do what you want to do. You two would be perfect together, and everyone deserves to be happy."

"Maybe I should talk to her about it—"

"No, just leave her alone. I know you guys are friends, but you're only friends with her because of me, so I don't think it really counts. I don't think it's the same thing as if I were to date Charlie...that would be weird."

"I guess I just feel bad because I know how she feels about him."

"Yeah. But they're never getting back together, so it really shouldn't matter." It would be a lot easier to talk Denise into this if I just told her the truth, but that wasn't an option. If Charlie wanted to tell her someday, that was his story to tell, not mine. "Go for it. Be happy. There's not a better guy out there."

"Not even Dax?" she teased.

"He's a perfect man—for me. But I don't think there's a better guy out there for you besides Charlie. I think he's exactly what you're looking for."

17

DAX

I approached the door and lightly tapped my knuckles against the wood.

"It's open." Carson's loud voice projected across the room and penetrated the barrier.

I stepped inside and saw the two of them working in the kitchen, making dinner. "Hey, sweetheart."

Charlie had his back to me as he stirred the contents on the stove. "Hey, pumpkin."

Carson turned around and rolled her eyes. A platter was in her hand, so she set it down before she came to me, that beautiful smile on her face.

Charlie quickly abandoned what he was doing and ran across the room to get to me quicker. He moved into my chest and gave me a bear hug, gripping me tightly like we were long-lost brothers who'd finally been reunited.

I chuckled and patted him on the back. "What's this for?"

He pulled away and gave me a dead serious look. "For getting her out of my apartment."

I chuckled. "You're welcome."

"Uh, what?" Carson said from behind him. "What the hell, Charlie?"

"You know how long it's been since I had sex on the couch?" He looked at her as he passed by her. "With you gone, there's going to be so much kitchen sex, couch sex…even closet sex, if you can believe it."

She crossed her arms over her chest and walked up to me. "He's going to miss me. Don't let him tell you any differently."

I glanced at him behind her.

He shook his head and got back to work on the stove.

I shifted my gaze back to her. "I'm sure he will, sweetheart."

She moved into my chest and wrapped her arms around me, rising on her tiptoes to kiss me.

My hands snaked down her back until I gripped both cheeks in my large hands. My palms were always on her ass, but she liked it, so I continued to do it.

She melted at my touch, like she loved those big fingertips digging into her jeans. "You want to join us for dinner?"

"Why do you think I'm here?"

She pulled away with accusation in her eyes. "I thought to see me."

"Of course, sweetheart. But if there's a home-cooked meal…"

She gave me a playful smack before we sat together at the dining table, the fajitas in the center of the table with warm tortillas. We scooped the sautéed veggies onto our flour tortillas and ate. Carson ate her food quickly like always, and Charlie was a little more graceful about it.

"So, when is this happening?" Charlie asked in between bites.

"When are you going to go for Denise?" Carson countered.

Charlie shifted his gaze to her. "You really want me to fuck your sister, huh?"

"Well, she deserves some good D," Carson said. "You give good D, right? Based on the noises I hear across the hallway, I'd say so. Plus, what Kat has said... So I want Denise to get her groove on, you know? Women should want other women to get good sex. It's just classy."

Everything that came out of her mouth amused me, so I smiled in between bites.

Charlie just looked at her like he had no idea what to say. "I'll go over there after dinner."

"To give her some D?" Carson asked in surprise.

"No," Charlie said quickly. "To see if she wants to start something up. I mean, if she wants to do that, I'm not going to say no, but that's not what I'm going for."

"Great." Carson turned back to her food. "It'll be nice to have the apartment to ourselves."

"Or you can just move out and have a whole penthouse to yourself," Charlie countered.

"Oh shut up." She balled up her napkin and threw it at him. "You don't want me to leave. You said on a scale of one to ten, you were going to miss me at a solid five."

Charlie looked at me and shook his head. "I don't remember saying that."

"You're so full of shit. You totally said it," Carson countered.

Charlie shrugged and kept eating.

I believed Carson on this one, because I couldn't imagine anyone wouldn't miss her. Her energy was infectious, and she always made everyone around her feel good. I felt lucky that I got to be the one to come home to her every single day.

"Seriously." Charlie looked at me. "When is she moving?"

I shrugged and turned to Carson. "Whenever she feels like it. I told her she can bring her furniture, but she said she didn't want to, so...it's just her clothes and stuff." They were things she could move in a few hours on a Saturday, but she hadn't done it yet.

Carson held my gaze while the fajita was in her hand. "It didn't seem like there was a rush, so I'm taking my time."

"Why?" Charlie countered. "You're moving in to a *penthouse*. Why are you taking your time?"

"Maybe because I want to spend a little more time with you...dumbass." She kept her eyes on her food as she kept eating.

Charlie watched her for a few seconds before a subtly soft look came over his face, like those words touched him. "I guess it wouldn't be the end of the world if you stuck around a little bit longer..."

"Getting cold feet?" I lay beside her in her small bed, right up against the window where the city lights came through the blinds. I was used to having a king-size bed all to myself, and now I shared a queen-size with Carson. But less space meant we were pressed closer together, so it wasn't all bad. I would never make Carson feel self-conscious for what she had, but I was eager for her to move in to my penthouse where it was always quiet, where we were elevated above the city, so bright lights didn't shine through the windows if we didn't want them to. There was a lot more room, and I didn't have to share the space with her roommate.

"No." She lay beside me with her leg hooked over my hip, her hand against my chest. "I've honestly just been so busy lately that the idea of organizing my stuff and making the move seems like too much."

I'd offer to pay people to do it for her, but I knew her well enough to know that was a bad suggestion.

"And spending another week with Charlie isn't so terrible. When I got married, I missed spending so much time with him, but I think this time, I won't miss him so much. Even if we stop working together, I'll still see him all the time. And I think he and Denise will probably get serious, so he won't have all the time to spend with me like he used to."

"Yeah."

"And we're going to have so much fun living together that he probably won't be on my mind much."

I smiled. "I'll make sure no one else is on your mind but me."

"Ooh...that sounds nice."

"I just want to make sure you don't feel pressured—"

"I don't," she said quickly. "If I did, trust me, I would tell you."

That was one of the best things about her, that she would speak her mind so there was never any misunderstanding. Her bluntness wasn't always polite, but it made my life much easier. "Good. Because I can't wait until you get your ass over to my place."

She smiled slightly. "I hope I don't turn into some stuck-up, rich bitch..."

"Never." She would never let her surroundings go to her head. She was too down-to-earth for that. "I can always help you move if you want."

"It's really not that much stuff, but I probably will need to borrow a truck or rent a moving van."

"The van sounds good. I can drive it for you if you want."

"That would be nice, since my driver's license expired and Charlie doesn't have one."

"Consider it done." If my friends knew I was driving a moving van around instead of hiring someone to do it, they would talk so much shit. "So, how about next Saturday?"

She considered it for a while before she nodded. "Sure. Saturday."

I'd finally gotten her on my line and reeled her in.

"I'll have everyone over, and we'll make a thing of it."

"Great. I'd like them to see my place since they're going to be over all the time," I said.

"I don't know about *all the time*..."

"Knowing you, yes, it'll be often. And I don't mind. Your

friends feel like my friends at this point."

"That's sweet." Her arm hooked around my neck, and she fingered my hair as she gave me a kiss. "Maybe I should try to be friendlier with your sister."

"Eh. You don't have to do that."

"You guys seem close."

"Doesn't mean you have to be. And I know your initial meeting wasn't all that great."

Her forehead rested against mine. "I don't hold grudges, so I don't think about that. She's your only surviving family member. It would be nice if we could be friends. You know, get our nails done, whatever girls do."

"You don't get your nails done."

She held out her hand and looked at her fingertips. "That's because I'm typing all the time, and they chip and stuff. I guess we can just drink together. That's something everyone can do."

I chuckled. "True."

A sad look suddenly came on to her face, like she was thinking of something particularly heartbreaking.

I suspected I knew what it was. "She'll come around. Give it time."

"Yeah..."

"And if she doesn't, it's her problem and not yours. I think she totally overreacted, and she needs to mature and grow up."

"That's a little harsh," she whispered.

"Or maybe someone needs to be straight with her."

"It's hard to be straight with someone when they're heartbroken."

"She shouldn't be heartbroken. They've been broken up for almost a year." Maybe I was being harsh, but it was only because I was biased toward Carson. She was the most amazing woman I'd ever met, and anyone who took her for granted was practically an enemy. "I'm just saying, if she's smart, she'll come around. And if not...that's not your problem."

18

CARSON

CHARLIE DIDN'T COME HOME THAT NIGHT.

During the week, he always made dinner. The only exception to that was Wednesday night, when we got pizza and wings after the game. Instead of waiting for him to come home, I prepared dinner for two and made him a plate so he would have it when he returned.

But the hours passed, and he never showed.

I texted him. *Hey, you alright?*

No response.

Charlie? I never checked in with him because he was a grown-ass man, but his behavior was peculiar. If he was out late on assignment, he usually told me where he was in case everything went south. He hadn't checked in. If he had a date, he usually shared that information with me so I wouldn't worry where he was all night.

Still nothing.

I'm starting to worry. Just let me know you're okay.

Thirty minutes went by and still no response.

Was I just being paranoid? What if there was really something wrong? It was past nine, and I wouldn't be able to sleep unless I knew he was okay. I decided to call.

It rang for a long time.

He answered just before I hung up. "Carson, I'm kinda busy right now..."

"Oh, thank god. I just wanted to check that you're okay. You've never not come home before without letting me know. Are you on assignment?"

"No. I'm with Denise..."

My eyes widened at the revelation, and I cupped my mouth even though my gasp was silent. "Ooh...gotcha. Give it to her good, alright? And make sure—"

He hung up.

I grinned and put the phone aside, relieved that he was totally fine and something was happening with Denise—finally. This narrative had been going on for a long time, and I was glad it had some kind of forward movement at last.

I texted Dax. *Charlie didn't come home tonight, so I started to worry. Guess what he's doing?*

I think you mean guess WHO he's doing. And I think that answer is obvious.

I can't believe it. Charlie and my sister.

I can't believe it took this long. So, you're alone for the rest of the night?

Looks like it.

You want company?

I'm just going to watch TV and go to bed.

Well...we could have couch sex.

Hmm...not a bad idea.

I'll be back there in twenty minutes, sweetheart.

Perfect. I'll put on some lingerie.

His response was lightning fast. *Make it ten minutes.*

"Spill it." I stepped into Charlie's cubicle and hopped onto his desk.

Charlie looked up from his laptop and gave me an incredulous look. "You know I don't kiss-and-tell."

My legs swayed back and forth as I raised an eyebrow. "Don't kiss-and-tell, my ass." He told me about every woman he'd been with, fingering a date in the back seat of a taxi and doing it on a deserted beach at Coney Island.

"But you don't *know* those women. You don't even know what they look like, just have a first name. This is different."

"At least that means there was some kissing not to tell."

He turned back to his computer and brushed off my interrogation.

"She's just going to tell me next time I see her, you know."

"And you don't think it's weird to hear the intimate details about your sister's sex life?" He turned in his chair and faced me.

"No." I shrugged. "I tell her stuff all the time. You've never told your brother about nailing some woman in the back of a club?"

His shrug was an affirmation. "We had a great time—I'll leave it at that." A slight smile spread on his lips, a look of happiness accompanying it in his eyes. Charlie had always been a positive person, but that smile made me realize how unhappy he'd been prior to this, and now...he was actually happy.

"Did you give her that D?"

He rolled his eyes.

I narrowed my eyes and stared at his face.

"Come on, I'm a gentleman."

"You wouldn't be the first guy she's slept with on the first date, so you don't need to protect her reputation. Come on, it's the twenty-first century."

He grinned. "Since you're going to pull it out of me...she got that D—and a lot of it."

"Woo-hoo!" I threw my hands in the air and made a scene, so the rest of the reporters turned to look at us.

"Shh!" Charlie slapped my knee.

I lowered my hands and dropped my voice. "I'm so happy for you guys. This was a long time coming."

"You're telling me..."

"You think she'll join us on the court for basketball?"

"Not sure. I think she likes watching me play instead." He waggled his eyebrows.

"I bet." I chuckled then got off the desk. "Well, I should get back to work. Simon Prescott isn't going to end up in jail by himself."

"Has he contacted you since?"

I shook my head. "Nope. I'm sure he's all talk."

"Still, keep your eyes peeled, alright? Never underestimate anyone, just as someone should never underestimate you."

I gave him a thumbs-up. "Good advice."

WHEN WE WALKED onto the court, I spotted Dax in his black running shorts, his perfectly chiseled torso shiny with sweat. He had those sexy narrow hips with the tight abs underneath his tanned skin, and his veins ran at the very bottom of his stomach along with a thin line of hair. His hands moved to his hips before he wiped his forehead with the back of his arm.

Charlie and Denise walked behind me and moved to the bleachers.

"Look at her drool." My sister took a seat and crossed her legs.

I snapped out of the stare and turned back to her. "Hey, you can't blame me."

Charlie pulled his shirt over his head.

Denise's eyes immediately went to his naked chest. "Yeah, I can't."

Charlie chuckled like he knew she was staring at him. "I'm

going to go warm up." He leaned down and gave her a peck on the lips before he jogged onto the court.

Denise checked out his ass before she looked at me.

I grinned. "I heard things got pretty heavy."

She flipped her hair behind her shoulder and played it cool. "Very."

"You guys are cute together."

"We are, aren't we?" She smiled. "And he's so smart and such a good guy. Way better than all the doctors and nurses I usually date. I feel like every time I dated a guy, it was just stuffy and forced, but with him, it just feels right."

Yeah, because the guy is head over heels in love with you. "Yeah, he's the best guy I know."

"The best?" Dax's playful voice came from behind me.

I grinned before I turned around. "Okay…second best."

He walked up to me, his chest sweaty and sexy. "That's better."

My fingertips went to his abs and felt the wet hardness as my eyes moved up his body, over his sexiness and to his face, where there was a nice shadow along his jawline. I rose on my tiptoes to kiss him, my hands grabbing on to his torso for balance. "You're so hot."

He smiled against my mouth as he kissed me. "You want to ditch the game and find an alleyway?"

"I mean…I wouldn't say no."

He chuckled before he kissed me again. "We'll find one on the way home." He pulled away and gave my ass a smack before he walked onto the court.

I walked with him.

"So…Charlie and Denise?"

"Yep. Charlie and Denise."

He looked at Charlie, who stood with his hands on his hips, but instead of focusing on the game, he was staring at Denise on the bleachers. "He looks happy."

"And she looks happy too."

He turned back to me. "Looks like you did good."

"Guess I'm cupid's little bitch now."

He chuckled before he joined his team on the other side of the half court line. "Ready, sweetheart?"

"Am I ready to kick your ass?" I asked. "Always." I blew him a kiss.

He caught it then flattened his palm over his crotch.

"Ooh, I like that."

CHARLIE HAD his arm around Denise's shoulders as he sat beside her in the booth, turning his head toward her often to stare at her face every time she talked, like watching her lips move was hypnotizing. "So, tonight's the last night…"

"Yep." I pulled my beer closer to me. "Our last night together."

Matt turned to Charlie. "You don't seem too sad about it."

Charlie pulled Denise closer to him and pressed a kiss to her hairline. "It's hard for me to be sad about anything lately."

Denise closed her eyes as she felt his affection, like his embrace gave her a high that couldn't be replicated with anything else.

"So, you're going to live in that apartment alone?" Matt asked. "It's a two-bedroom."

"I'm not going to move just because Carson is leaving," Charlie answered. "I can make rent on my own."

"Even without me paying for all the groceries?" I questioned.

"As long as you don't keep eating half my lunch every day, I should be able to do it," Charlie countered. "And we know I don't need condoms anymore, so…that's a nice savings."

Matt winked before he gave him a thumbs-up.

"You're the one going to save a ton on everything," Charlie

said. "No rent. No groceries. You should invest that money and turn it into some serious cash flow."

"What are you talking about?" I asked. "I'll still pay rent and stuff. I'm not a freeloader."

"You think you can pay half the mortgage?" Charlie asked incredulously. "It's probably like $100,000 or something."

"I can pay what I'm paying now." I drank from my beer.

"And you think he's just going to take it?" Matt asked. "That doesn't make any sense."

We hadn't really talked about it, so I had no idea. "I'm sure there are things I can chip in for."

"Or you could just buy lingerie," Charlie said. "Dax will love seeing your selection in his closet every day."

I rolled my eyes and kept drinking.

"Oh, there he is." Matt gave a deep sigh. "Looking all sexy as usual."

I turned to watch him walk inside, wearing his suit because he was meeting up with us after work. Perfect from head to toe, he was one hell of a man. "Yep..." I gave a sigh too, like he was tender meat I could sink my teeth into.

When Dax spotted us, he came over and slid into the booth beside me. "Hey, sweetheart." His arm moved around my shoulders, and he leaned in to give me a kiss.

I kissed him deeply right in front of my friends, not caring if they stared.

When we pulled back, he squeezed my thigh under the table.

"She hasn't even started packing yet." Charlie threw me under the bus right away.

"I'll do it tonight. Chill," I insisted. "I procrastinate on *everything*."

"Don't expect me to help you," Charlie said. "You always wait until the last minute for everything and assume I'll come to the rescue."

"I'll help her," Denise said. "We can drink wine and go

through her clothes, and if I see something I like, I'll borrow it."

I rolled my eyes. "So selfless of you."

We continued to chat at the table after Dax got his drink. Charlie and Denise were across from us, and Matt was at the head of the booth. We talked about basketball, the status of Matt's relationship with Jeremy, and work.

"I can't wait to see your place," Charlie said. "I've never been in a penthouse before."

"Me too," Matt said. "I bet we could all live there, and you wouldn't even notice us."

I gave Matt a cold look. "Take it down a notch, alright?" I was sure Dax didn't want people to obsess over how rich he was.

"It's fine," Dax said with a chuckle. "I'm excited for you guys to come over. I'm sure we'll have lots of game nights."

"Sweet," Matt said.

"Carson is under the impression that she'll be paying her fair share while she's there." Charlie glanced at me. "Which is ridiculous."

"It's not ridiculous," I countered. "I'm a working woman. I should pay for stuff."

"You can pay with sex," Dax said. "That's as good as cash, if you ask me."

Charlie chuckled before he fist-bumped Dax across the table.

I wouldn't be a freeloader. That wasn't my style. "That's not who I am—"

"Uh, guys..." Matt's face turned pale as milk as he looked across the bar.

"What?" I asked, following his gaze to see what affected him so deeply.

Everyone else turned too.

Kat stood there with another girl, probably a friend from work, and she looked at us with vacant eyes, like her soul had escaped through her pores and she was empty inside. Her stare was focused on Charlie with his arm around Denise. Her hair was pulled back from her face in a ponytail, so every expression was visible like words on a page.

Dax released a quiet sigh, like he could feel her pain.

Charlie dropped his arm from Denise's shoulder—as if that would make a difference.

Then Kat quickly stormed out and pushed through the double doors until she was outside.

Charlie's previous happiness was long gone, replaced by self-loathing. "Fuck. I'll go talk to her."

"No." I tapped Dax on the arm so he would get up. "Let me try. I don't think she'd feel comfortable looking at you right now."

Dax quickly got out of the way so I could cross the bar and head outside. I found her down the sidewalk, walking quickly in her heels with her hand raised to get the attention of a cab. I was in flats, so I jogged to catch up to her and made it just when a taxi pulled over. "Kat."

She opened the back door.

I slammed my palm into it and closed it again.

The driver started to honk.

"Kat, talk to me—"

"And say what?" With watery eyes and a loud voice, she rounded on me, like everything she kept inside had burst free. "That I mean literally nothing to all of you, not just Charlie? Seeing you guys having a good time, all happy, just makes me realize that you've already forgotten me. I remember when it used to be the four of us before Denise moved here, and that was my life. It used to be the four of us, his arm around *my* shoulders...and now I've been replaced. And it wasn't just Charlie who replaced me—all of you did."

"That's not true—"

"You guys all have forgotten me. And that's fine." She tried to open the door again.

I put my weight against it so she couldn't open it. "Kat, I love you. I'm still your best friend. I think about you every day because I miss you. I'm sorry that we look like we're happy without you, but we all miss you. I'm not lying to you."

With tears dripping down her cheeks, she stared at the cab as she waited for me to move my hand.

The driver honked again.

"Oh, shut it!" I yelled.

Kat's voice was quiet now, like she'd given up. "Move your hand, Carson."

"Kat, come back inside. We'll show you how much we miss you."

"You expect me to go in there and watch Charlie love her the way he used to love me?" She turned to me, her eyes red and irritated.

"I expect you to make an effort for us to stay friends, because no matter what happens, we're all friends. I know this is hard for you and I can't even imagine how you must feel, but our friendship is so important. We should all be together."

She turned back to the cab and pushed my arm down.

This time, I stopped fighting. "I still need you, Kat. My life isn't the same without you." I put my heart out there, vulnerable and bare, but it wasn't enough.

She got into the cab and left.

I GRABBED the clothes off the hangers and folded them before placing them in one of the boxes.

Denise helped organize my things while Dax leaned against the headboard on the bed, his ankles crossed at the edge. Charlie leaned against the wall with his head tilted back, looking at the light fixture in the center of the room. Matt stood in the doorway.

My bedroom was way too small for five people, but we crowded inside anyway.

I kept working like nothing happened.

"I don't know what to do," Charlie whispered. "Our conversation seemed to go well."

Denise had her head down, like she felt personally responsible for everything.

"I'm sure it was totally different to actually see it happen in the flesh." I pulled down another sweater and folded it before I handed it to Denise. "I think we've done everything we can do. I told her how much we love and miss her, but she just…" I shrugged and turned back to the closet to grab the next sweater. "I don't think there's anything else we can do. Just have to let it be."

Charlie sighed from the floor. "I'm sorry, Carson…"

"Don't be." I grabbed a couple more items then handed them to Denise. "You deserve to be happy. You shouldn't have to apologize for that. You did everything you could have possibly done to prevent this, so maybe there was nothing any of us could ever do." I was sad that I'd lost my friend and it would hurt for a long time, but I also accepted the fact that there was nothing more I could do, nothing anyone could do.

It is what it is.

"I texted her the other day, and she didn't even text me back," Matt said. "And I have nothing to do with any of this. It seems like she's the one not making the effort. From my point of view, we did everything we could to make this work. She's the one who just refuses to see that."

After my clothes were gone from the closet, it was totally empty.

And it was a strange sight.

The last time one of my closets was empty like this, I'd moved in with Evan.

But I knew this time when I left, I wouldn't come back.

It was different with Dax.

"Looks like the closet is done." I turned back to them and approached the dresser. "We're making good time. I guess procrastinating isn't the worst thing in the world." I spoke to a room full of people, but it felt empty, because they couldn't brush off what happened either.

Dax got off the bed then came to me, wrapping his arms around me and pressing his face into the crook of my neck. "It'll be alright, sweetheart. Someway, somehow, it'll be alright."

WE GOT everything into the back of the van that was parked at the curb outside my building. Once all of my stuff was gathered and put into one spot, I realized how little I actually had. Some of my things had been left behind at Evan's place because I didn't want anything that reminded me of him.

Matt stared at the van before he turned to Dax, who was in sweatpants and a t-shirt that looked tight over his strong muscles. "So, you're going to drive *that* to your place?"

"Yes," Dax said with a grin. "I've driven a vehicle before."

It was big and boxy and had an obnoxious logo along the side. I grinned. "It's not a Bugatti, but you'll still look hot driving it."

"Whoa, what?" Matt asked. "You have a Bugatti?"

I gave him a glare. "Matt."

Dax held up his two fingers. "Two. One in black—and one in red." He moved to the driver's side door.

Matt looked like he wanted to faint.

"We'll pile up in the back so we can all go together." Charlie was in his workout clothes, and so was Denise.

"Is that safe?" Matt asked.

"We're going like ten blocks." Denise got into the back and sat on one of the boxes. "It'll be fine."

Charlie joined her and then Matt.

I walked to the doors so I could close them.

Matt glanced at the front where Dax was getting his safety belt on. "You think he'll give me a ride sometime—"

I shut the doors in his face then got into the passenger seat.

"Ready?" Dax turned the key in the ignition and got the engine going.

"Yep," I said. "Looks like I'm your copilot."

Effortlessly, he merged into traffic and drove through the city without even having a back window. He didn't seem flustered at all, driving the huge boxy truck through town. He even placed one hand on my hip as he maintained control of the vehicle with the other.

"Thanks for doing this," I said.

"No problem, sweetheart." He looked at me, wearing that handsome smile. "Thanks for moving in with me."

"I think I'm the one who should be thanking you. I get to live with a super-hot guy."

"True." He looked ahead, still grinning. "And I usually do fifty push-ups the second I get out of bed."

"Ooh...I've never seen that."

"Because I'm too busy paying attention to you."

"Wow, I should have moved in sooner."

He chuckled and kept driving.

We eventually pulled up to his building, and the two doormen stared at us like we didn't belong there at all. They were both wearing stuffy suits with bowler hats. But when Dax got out, their demeanors completely changed.

I opened the back doors so everyone could come out.

Matt turned to me. "Did you ask him about the Bugatti?"

I rolled my eyes and handed him a box. "I'm not going to ask him that."

"I'd be happy to give you a ride, Matt." Dax came around the other side, not the least bit bothered by my friend's obsession. "We'll take it out of the city so we can really get some speed. I might even let you drive a little bit."

Matt almost dropped the box. "I think I might love you."

Dax chuckled then grabbed a box to carry inside.

I smacked Matt when Dax walked away. "Tone it down, would you?"

"What?" Matt snapped. "Like he doesn't already know."

We all grabbed a couple things and carried them inside the building. We all got into the elevator and rose to his penthouse, where the double doors opened to reveal his luxurious living room. I told them to be cool about it, but that didn't happen at all.

All three of them stood there with wide-open eyes, like they couldn't believe what they were looking at.

Dax stepped out of the elevator first to carry the box down the hallway.

"Holy shit," Charlie said. "Just his living room is bigger than our apartment."

I ignored the comment and stepped inside.

Matt spoke to Charlie. "I can't believe Carson gets to live here."

I turned around and looked at him. "I'm moving here because of Dax—not where he lives."

Charlie stepped farther inside and scanned the area, checking out the eighty-inch TV on the wall and all the paintings. "Yeah, but...still. You're one lucky-ass bitch."

AFTER WE PUT ALL the boxes in the bedroom and Dax dropped off the van, we gathered in the living room for sandwiches, chips, and drinks. The TV was on and played the game. We were tired from moving all day, but once we had some food in our stomachs, we started to lighten up.

"So, is it weird that you won't be going back to the apartment after this?" Charlie asked as he stuffed his hand into his bag of chips.

I took a look around at the spacious place, the full kitchen that could easily be used to cook a feast for twenty people. The dining table had a glorious view of the city, so I could sit there and write in the evenings as I watched the lights from the buildings. "A bit. But it also feels like home."

Dax sat beside me and placed his hand on my thigh as he leaned in to give me a kiss on the corner of the mouth. "It feels more like home to me than it ever has before."

"Give it some time," Charlie said ominously. "Good thing you have a housekeeper."

"Might need to hire a second one," Denise teased.

Matt held up three fingers. "Make it three."

I rolled my eyes as they teased me. "They're exaggerating."

"Wouldn't care if they weren't." His arm moved around my shoulders, and he pulled me close, looking at me like I was the most important thing in the world. His love felt real, unconditional, like there was nothing I could ever do to make him stop loving me.

My eyes softened.

"I love you." His hand moved into the back of my hair as he cradled my face close. He spoke quietly but still loud enough for them to hear, wearing his heart on his sleeve like a real man, like he didn't care if people heard his declaration of love.

I kissed him on the mouth for a bit before I pulled away. "I love you too."

His other hand grabbed mine on my thigh. With his eyes on me, he gently opened my fingers before he placed something small in the center. Then he wrapped my fingers around it, making it a closed fist.

All my friends gasped.

I felt the key to his penthouse in my grip, the warm metal the same temperature as my skin. My fingers squeezed it tighter, but that was when I realized it wasn't a key at all.

I inhaled a deep breath when I figured out what it was.

He kept his focused gaze on me, his look intense like it was in the bar the night we met. "Will you marry me?"

My head immediately dropped as my fingers opened, seeing the diamond ring he'd placed there.

"Oh my god," Matt whispered.

It was a simple band with a single diamond in the center. It wasn't a big diamond that a billionaire would buy his trophy wife. It was small and humble, just like me. He'd picked out a ring I would want, not an obnoxious rock that would just get in my way.

I lifted my head and looked at him again.

He waited for my answer, confident that he already knew what I would say.

He didn't take me to a fancy restaurant or on a luxury trip to propose. He asked me exactly how I would want to be asked, unexpectedly and with my friends there to celebrate. He truly understood who I was and never tried to change me, even when he didn't always agree.

I opened my fingers again, grabbed the ring, and slipped it onto my ring finger.

His lips slowly lifted into a smile.

My hands cupped his cheeks, and I kissed him. "Yes," I whispered against his mouth, listening to my friends clap and cheer.

"Aw," Denise said. "That was so sweet..."

Matt whistled.

I knew that meant I'd have to walk away from the job that I loved, but it was a compromise I was willing to make for this man. Truly, I didn't feel like I was losing anything, but gaining something better. I wouldn't have to fall so far as to take on the Lifestyle section, though it would be a big change of pace. But he would make up for all the excitement that I was leaving behind.

When Dax pulled away, his smile was gone, and now he looked at me with emotional eyes, like he'd just gotten everything he'd ever wanted. His fingers moved into my hair and pulled it from my face, his palm cupping my cheek as he regarded me. "Carson Frawley...sounds right."

"What makes you think I'd change my last name?" I teased.

"Because it sounds so hot."

"Yeah." I gave a slight nod. "It does sound pretty hot."

19

DAX

I'D ASKED SOMEONE TO MARRY ME BEFORE. I'D PICKED out the ring, planned how I'd ask the question, so the novelty should be gone.

But it felt like the first time.

Because this time, it was right.

Carson was the one.

The food was left on the coffee table in the living room, and her boxes were stacked near the windows in my bedroom to be unpacked later. We were in bed, making love, enjoying each other as fiancés.

With her thighs squeezing my hips, I rocked into her, seeing the shine of sweat on her forehead from the lights coming through the window. Her green eyes were lit up with their own illumination, the fire burning in her soul. Her fingers dug into my slightly damp hair as she rocked back with me, the metal from her ring coming into contact with my skin.

She pulled me close as she started to writhe, her back arching, her head rolling back, her toes curling against my ass. Her nails dug into my flesh as she dragged them down the back of my neck, the sweat burning the openings as it poured inside. "Yes..."

The only thing better than having an orgasm was watching her have one. She tightened around me like she did all the other times, her wetness soaking into my shaft because she exploded with arousal. She moaned louder and louder until her hips bucked uncontrollably as she hit the crescendo.

I slammed into her over and over, hitting her hard and driving her into the fireworks, watching her hit the high and slowly come down as I reached the finish line. I filled her for the fifth time that night, the hour unknown because we'd knocked over the clock at some point in the rendezvous.

I wanted to keep going, but I was on empty.

She probably was too.

I rolled off her and lay there, staring at the ceiling, catching my breath, feeling the sweat slowly evaporate from my skin.

She breathed hard beside me as her body slowly sank into a state of calm. Naked on top of my sheets, her body was beautiful, her tits perfect, her lithe stomach irresistible. Her hair looked like it'd been struck by a tornado, but that only made her more irresistible.

My hand snaked to hers on the bed, and I interlocked our fingers.

She turned her head to look at me, a slight smile coming onto her lips.

I pulled her hand and rested it on my chest so she could feel my steady heartbeat. She made it race when she touched me, but in our quiet moments, she brought me so much peace, brought the crazy world to a standstill.

"Did they know you were going to ask?" she whispered.

I whispered my response. "No."

"Good. Those idiots can't keep a secret."

I chuckled. "I wanted to make sure you were surprised."

"Mission accomplished."

I wasn't afraid that she would say no. The fact that she'd agreed to move in with me, agreed to take a step back at her job to be with me, told me that she was in this forever, that she wanted to love me until we were buried beside each other. "Do you like the ring?"

She scrunched up her face and gave a disbelieving reaction. "Do I like the gorgeous ring you got for me?" She held up her left hand so she could see the diamond. "Yes. I love it. It's perfect for me."

I knew she wouldn't want an enormous rock like most women. She'd want something nice but simple, something she could wear everywhere.

"But I like the man who gave it to me more."

I brought her hand to my lips and kissed it.

"You knew I'd say yes?"

"Without a doubt." I stared into her eyes, feeling that connection between our souls, the unconditional love that would last forever. Fifty percent of marriages ended in divorce. Our first marriages ended, and that meant this one wouldn't. This time, it was right.

Her eyes lit up.

I was happy. Really happy. Happier than I'd ever been.

"I hope you didn't ask me to marry you so I'd leave my job quicker."

"No. I said when we get married, so you have some time."

"Well, I don't think there's much of a difference between fiancés and husband and wife. I'll tell Vince on Monday."

That was exactly what I wanted, but I hid my joy. "What will you do now?"

"There are still a lot of options for me. Editorial pieces, different kinds of investigative journalism, just stuff less dangerous. I have a good relationship with my editor, so he'll give me something decent. I won't be booted back to the Lifestyle section."

I chuckled. "Is the Lifestyle section really that bad?"

"No. Just not for me."

I turned over onto my side so I could be closer to her. "I really appreciate that you're willing to do that for me, for us."

When she looked at me, there wasn't a hint of resentment, like she agreed that it was the best decision. "I know better than anybody how dangerous that job is, and when it's just me, that's not a big deal. But when I think about having a family and stuff, I feel differently about it. I never seriously considered it before, because it seemed like it would never become a reality. But now it feels real, so it could happen."

I was glad she thought that way, thought about more than just us, but our future family. "We're going to have a good life together."

"I know." She came closer to me and ran her fingers down my arm. "And not just because you have two Bugattis."

I chuckled.

"I'm sorry about Matt. He's just—"

"It really doesn't bother me. Your friends are harmless."

"*Our* friends."

I smiled. "Yes…ours."

"So…" She hooked her leg over my hip. "I'm not sure what you're thinking, but I did the full-on wedding before and I'm just not really into that…unless that's important to you."

I shook my head. "Now that my parents are gone, not really."

"You want to do something small, then?"

"Yes. We can even go down to city hall if you want."

"And get sandwiches afterward?" she said with a smile.

"Doesn't sound bad to me."

"I just want to wear a wedding dress. Whether we go to city hall or have a ceremony, I want to look beautiful, you know?"

"And you'll look fiiiiine in a wedding dress."

She smiled. "Especially in a low-cut one with a high slit up the side."

"And lingerie underneath."

"Ooh, even better."

"When did you want to do this?"

She shrugged. "When did you want to do this?"

I'd marry her tomorrow or a year from now. "The ball is in your court, sweetheart. We both know I would have married you tonight if that's what you wanted. So, I'll let you decide."

"All up to me, huh?" she whispered.

"No pressure. We can be engaged for years, and then if you suddenly get the urge, we can walk down and do it. Just in the moment."

"I don't want to be engaged for *years*."

"Then, a year?"

She shrugged. "We're already living together, so..."

"Meaning?"

"Why don't we get married in a month or something?"

I really liked that answer.

"We've both done this before, and we both know this is right. Why wait?"

Couldn't agree more. "You don't need to live with me first to make sure you can tolerate me?"

"*Tolerate you?*" she said with a laugh. "Have you not heard all the horror stories my friends have told? I'm the tornado that's going to rip this penthouse apart."

"I like a challenge, so that works for me."

"It's nice to be with a man who can handle my craziness."

I smiled. "It's nice to be with a sexy, crazy-ass bitch."

She laughed loudly, loving the way I described her. "That's the most romantic thing anyone has ever said to me."

"Yeah?" I moved slightly on top of her so I could look down at her beautiful face and watch her continue to laugh. "I meant it."

She cupped my face as her laughter subsided and her eyes warmed. "I know you do."

"Geez, what happened?" Renee stood in front of my desk and looked down at me.

I lifted my chin and looked at her. "Sorry?"

"You look like a fucking clown right now." She made a big smile, showing all her teeth with her eyes wide. "Why are you smiling like that?"

"Because I'm happy, dumbass." I rose from my chair and smoothed out my tie as I looked at my sister.

"But you're, like, really happy. Crazy happy."

I slid my hands into my pockets and considered how I would tell her.

"You really like Carson living with you, huh?"

"It's not just that."

"Then what?"

"I asked her to marry me—and she said yes."

Her jaw immediately dropped, and her lips parted in shock. "Oh my god…"

"Yep." I didn't have any fear that the past would repeat itself, that I'd made another wrong decision. Carson should have been my wife in the first place. If only I'd met her sooner. "That crazy-ass bitch is going to be your sister-in-law."

She was still in shock. "I just had no idea that's where your head was at."

"It's been that way since the moment I met her, honestly. I told you she was the one."

"But I didn't expect you to propose so quickly…after everything that happened."

"It's different this time. I'm not worried about it."

She regained her composure and crossed her arms over her chest. "Well, I'm happy for you. It's been a long time since you've been happy."

"Thanks, sis."

"So, you're going to get married in a year or something? Big wedding? Am I going to be a bridesmaid?"

"No, we aren't doing that. Neither one of us cares for that. Just going to go down to city hall in a month."

Now Renee looked shocked all over again. "In a month?"

I started to hear the rain behind me, pelting the windows with drops that created elemental background music. "Yes."

"You don't think that's fast?" she asked hesitantly. "You've known her for what...six months?"

"When you know, you know."

Renee still looked visibly uncomfortable, like she might vomit.

"I didn't realize you still disliked Carson." Whether Renee liked her or not, it wouldn't change my decision. Carson was the only woman in this world who would make me happy. I wouldn't let her go. My sister would just have to change her opinion.

"It's not that I dislike her. It's just... I don't want the past to repeat itself."

"It won't."

"So, you're getting a prenup?" she asked. "I guess if you do that, it's fine. I just worry that it's happening too fast and she's got her eyes on the money, but if you do all the paperwork, it shouldn't matter if her motives are less than genuine."

My eyes narrowed because I was immediately offended by every word that came out of her mouth. "I know I fucked up with Rose, but Carson is nothing like that. That's not even a concern."

"And I'm sure you're right, but half of this company is mine, and I don't want to share with it with *another* person. Are you telling me you aren't planning on getting the prenup?" Her eyebrows immediately rose in surprise.

Honestly, it hadn't crossed my mind. I didn't think it was necessary. Carson and I were going to be together forever, and even if we weren't, she'd probably sign everything to me because she wouldn't want it anyway. She wasn't that kind of person.

Her eyes narrowed. "Dax?"

"I hadn't really thought about it, honestly."

Her visage completely changed, like she was disappointed in me. "You're joking."

"Carson isn't like that—"

"You've been wrong before," she snapped. "And even if you aren't, people change. She could get used to the wealthy lifestyle and change her feelings about it. This doesn't just affect you. It also affects me. You think I'd marry William without a prenup even though he's harmless? No one gets married thinking they're going to get divorced, but a lot of people do get a divorce. If Carson is really who you say she is, then she should have no problem signing those papers. She'll put her money where her mouth is."

I knew she would. I just didn't want to ask.

"I can't believe, after everything we've been through, you would be so stupid."

I dropped my gaze, heartbroken by her disappointment.

"Get that prenup, Dax." She turned away to leave my office. "Or I'll never look at you the same."

I MET with Charlie after work, and we got a beer at our usual place.

"I'm surprised you want to see me instead of your fiancée..."

"I wanted to talk to you about something...in private." He was the best person to ask because he was so close to Carson.

"Alright. If you're asking for my permission, it's a little late for that." He smiled like he was teasing and then took a drink of his beer. "And I'm happy to get rid of her, especially if you're the one taking her. Today, she told Vince that she wanted to be taken off the pharmaceutical piece and to take a step out of the fast lane. He was shocked...but understood."

I hadn't had a chance to talk to her today, and I was surprised she'd made the decision so quickly. Since she always procrastinated, I'd expected her to procrastinate about this. "How is she?"

"She said she's totally fine. Still seemed really happy."

That meant the world to me. "Where's she going to be working now?"

"She'll still be in the same office. She's going to do the big interviews with celebrities and influential people, so it's kind of a promotion anyway...just less dangerous."

I smiled. "That's great news."

"I suspect Vince had been planning to promote somebody else and give them that position, but he changed his mind when Carson said she would be taking a step back. He's really fond of her, so he obviously doesn't want to lose her."

"Can't blame him."

He took a drink. "So everything's good. What did you want to talk about?"

For a second, I'd forgotten about my dilemma. "Can this stay between us?"

He turned serious at the question. "Depends on what you want to talk about. You know where my loyalty lies."

"It's something I'll have to talk to her about, regardless. I'm just running it by you first."

He nodded. "Then I guess it's okay."

I felt like a dick for even saying this out loud. "I need to ask Carson to sign a prenup. How do you think she'll react?"

Both of his eyebrows jumped up on his face. "That's it? That's what you're worried about?"

"It's a pretty controversial subject."

"Not to Carson. She'll totally understand. She won't even think twice about it."

"But asking her to do that implies two things. One, I think there's a chance we won't stay together forever. And two, I think she's going to steal all my money. That's not exactly romantic and how I want to start this relationship. It's not even a relationship—it's a marriage."

"I get what you're saying, but Carson won't see it that way. She understands it's just business. She's around people like this all the time, she gets it. Since she couldn't care less about your money, she's not going to hesitate to sign. She knows what you've been through already. You're overthinking it, man."

The weight left my shoulders, and I felt a million times lighter. If it were just me, I might not do the prenup, but the fact that it affected my sister made me feel differently. By not asking Carson to sign it, I felt like it was a declaration of my love for her, that after what Rose did to me, I completely trusted her. It was a testament to what we had. I felt like shit that I couldn't give that to her, that I couldn't prove my love in a really powerful way.

"Do you feel better?"

I nodded.

"Good. When she and Evan got divorced, she didn't take any of his money. He wasn't a billionaire, but he had quite a bit of assets. She just doesn't think that way. That's not who she is."

"I know. That's why I didn't want to ask her to sign anything—because I trust her implicitly."

He shrugged. "You've got a lot of assets to protect, not to mention the runaround Rose gave you before. Asking Carson to waive her rights to your wealth is not ridiculous. Don't stress about it. It's not going to affect your relationship at all."

I nodded before I finally took a drink of my beer. "You're right. She will understand."

"She'll totally understand. With absolutely no resentment."

I nodded again.

"Now go back to being ridiculously happy. I prefer you better when you have a stupid smile on your face."

I released a light chuckle, my body relaxing now that the

subject changed. "You have the same stupid smile too, you know."

"Oh, I do know. It's nice."

"How's the apartment?"

"Even nicer." He grinned before he took a drink of his beer. "It's nice to have my own space. Denise is her sister, so it's best to keep those two separate."

"Yeah."

"But I think tomorrow I'm going to try to talk to Kat again."

Honestly, I'd forgotten about her. I was so happy with Carson that Kat wasn't on my mind. Carson seemed happy too, like she hadn't been thinking about the situation either. "Do you think that'll do any good?"

"I have to try. I think if she knew that Carson was engaged, she might feel differently. Girls get emotional over stuff like that."

"That's true."

"And if she does nothing, I just won't mention it to Carson. But hopefully it'll make a difference."

I had all the money in the world, so I could give Carson anything she wanted. But I was powerless to give her the one thing that actually mattered to her.

Hopefully Charlie could. "Good luck."

"Thanks. I'm going to need it."

20

CHARLIE

When I arrived at her doorstep, I felt helpless. The whole thing seemed pointless, so I'd already accepted the defeat. But I had to try anyway.

For Carson.

I knocked on the door loudly and waited.

Her movements were audible in the apartment, her bare feet thudding against the rug and then turning silent when she was in front of the door.

I wondered if she would just walk away and ignore me.

She opened it.

She kept her hand on the door as she stared at me, not nearly as angry as she was when she spotted us in the bar last week. Maybe some time had cooled her off, and now she was just in pain. "What do you want?"

"To talk to you, if that's okay."

"I don't know what there is to say, Charlie. You and Denise are happy together, and that's fine. I really don't want to talk about it for an hour."

Now that I was finally with Denise and I was really happy, it dispelled my regret about meeting Denise when she moved here. However, it did make me regret being with Kat in the first place. While Kat was important to me and I loved her, I never felt with her what I did with Denise.

Denise would be my wife...someday.

But I would never tell Kat that. "I understand things are complicated now and it's difficult for you. But we are all still friends if you want to be. You have to take that chance now because it may not come again."

She crossed her arms over her chest, becoming guarded.

"You're important to all of us, and we want you back in our lives. You haven't been replaced. You haven't been forgotten. But we also can't change what happened. We can never make it better. And we're gonna eventually stop trying."

She dropped her gaze.

"I'm not going to come back here again and try to talk you into coming back. Carson isn't going to come either. We can't make you do anything you don't want to do, and if that's how you really feel, I don't know what we can do to change it."

"So, you came here to tell me this is my last chance?"

I shook my head. "No. I came here to tell you that Dax and Carson are engaged."

She quickly lifted her chin and looked at me, the emotional response undeniable.

"Carson is really happy, and I know she would be even happier if you were there for her right now. We're moving on with our lives, and you're going to miss it if you stay away. I don't know if that changes anything, but I thought you should know. Carson has always been there for you, and now it's time for you to be there for her and celebrate this moment with all of us."

She seemed to have been struck speechless because she didn't say anything. Her hand rubbed her other arm as she digested the news that her former best friend was getting married.

"We're going to do something simple for the ceremony in

about a month. I know it would mean a lot to Carson if you were there. But if you aren't there, I don't think anything will ever be the same again. So if you still value your friendships and are willing to push through everything, this is the time. You're on the clock."

21

CARSON

It was a big change, going from my apartment to a penthouse.

But it didn't feel weird because I already spent a lot of time there. Whenever I came home and he wasn't home from work, I didn't feel like I was in his space, but my space.

Our space.

I raided the fridge and made a snack and sat with my computer at the dining table. I was definitely cleaner and more organized than I used to be because I wanted to respect his space and our relationship. But maybe in a few years, I would go back to my old ways.

I handed all my paperwork and information about Kerosene Pharmaceuticals back to Vince so he could give it to a different reporter. It was a little hard to give up all my research, but I knew I was doing it for a good reason.

It didn't feel like a sacrifice, but rather a compromise.

Besides, my new assignment was still interesting. I would interview celebrities and influential people, write editorial pieces that exposed people on a deeper level. It had nothing to do with crime or scandals, but it was still a respectable line of work.

I was grateful.

And I would still get to see Charlie every day, so that was a plus.

Now that there wasn't so much urgency to do research, my mind wandered, and I looked at wedding dresses online.

The elevator beeped before the doors opened, and Dax walked inside wearing his suit. He had a satchel over his shoulder with his laptop and paperwork. Tall, strong, and sexy, he looked like a powerhouse in that suit.

Seeing that man every day I came home from work was not a bad way to live my life.

His eyes softened when he looked at me at the dining table. "This is nice." He approached the table as he slid his hands into his pockets. "Seeing you right when I walk in the door."

"I feel the same way."

He leaned down and kissed me, giving me seductive and slow kisses that made my body melt. He straightened before he pulled out the chair and took the seat beside me. "How was your day?"

"Good. I told Vince I wanted to be reassigned."

He gave a slight nod but didn't look surprised. "And you're okay with that?"

I nodded. "My first interview is with the prime minister of France, so not bad." I turned my open laptop so he could see my web browser. "I got kind of distracted, but I'll get back to work eventually." I closed it and pushed it aside.

He smiled with those dark eyes instead of his lips. "That makes me happy."

"The lingerie I pick out will make you happy too."

Now he did grin with his lips. "I'm sure it will."

"And how was your day, *honey*?" I spoke to him like a doting wife.

He moved his hands to the surface of the table and then

interlocked his fingers, displaying his expensive watch. "It was okay. I told Renee."

"Judging from your tone, it doesn't sound like a happy announcement." Yes, I wanted his sister to like me, but I wouldn't lose sleep if she didn't.

He stared out the window for a few seconds before he turned to me. "I don't want to have this conversation at all, especially so quickly into this engagement. But since you want to get married within a month, we should talk about it."

"Okay..."

He sighed before he looked at me again. "I need you to sign a prenup. Is that a problem?"

I narrowed my eyes at the question. "I already assumed that I would." I knew all the shit Rose had put him through, and since I wasn't a gold digger, I couldn't care less about waiving my rights to his wealth.

His neck suddenly stopped looking so tight, like this had been stressing him out all day. "I'm sorry I even have to ask you this..."

"Don't be." My hand moved to his wrist, and I gave him a squeeze. "I don't take it personally. I'm happy to sign it. Because I want to marry you—not your wallet."

The look he gave me was indescribable, like no one had ever said anything that affected him so deeply. There was affection and love, but something even deeper than that. His hand moved to mine, and he gave it a squeeze in return. "I love you...so fucking much."

WHEN I LEFT THE OFFICE, I waved down a cab. When a taxi pulled over, I opened the back door and took a seat.

There was someone already sitting next to the other window, a man I didn't want to see. "Hey, Carson." Simon

Prescott was in a three-piece suit, much too large to be crammed into the back of that small taxi.

The driver didn't pull away or ask for my address, so he was obviously paid to do what Simon told him to do.

My heart fluttered because I was caught off guard, but I gave him a cold stare like I was fearless and unaffected by the orchestrated visit. "How's killing innocent people going?"

He didn't react to my jab. "Business is good. Thanks for asking."

The best way to control the situation was to behave like you were the one in power, even if you weren't. So I took charge of the conversation, took the lead so he wouldn't feel like he had me cornered. "How can I help you?"

"I wanted to commend you for making the right choice. Killing you would've been such a waste, and I'm so glad I didn't have to."

I didn't know how he figured out so quickly that I'd stepped down, but my eyes narrowed in irritation because my decision had nothing to do with him or his threats. "I didn't walk away because of you. Let's get that straight. Your ego doesn't need another boost."

"There's no shame in admitting you value your life more than an article."

"Trust me, I would've chased you to the end of the earth if I didn't have a more pressing obligation."

"What obligation could possibly be more pressing than locking up an asshole like me?" He tilted his head as he regarded me, like my responses were truly interesting.

"Family." I would have a husband soon enough, maybe a couple kids in a few years. I couldn't risk my life anymore, not when I had someone who couldn't live without me.

"Again, you made the right choice. I suggest you warn whoever takes your place."

"Oh, I will." I grabbed the handle and opened the door. "Goodbye, Simon." I stepped out of the cab.

"Hopefully we'll cross paths again...under better circumstances."

I sat with Charlie in his cubicle, and we talked quietly so we wouldn't interrupt anybody nearby. "He acted like he was ready for me to throw a hissy fit when he asked me to sign a prenup. I'm surprised he would assume I would have a problem with it."

"I don't think that's what he assumed. He just wanted to make sure it wasn't going to be a problem."

"After everything that happened with his ex, I really can't blame him. Even if that never happened at all, I still wouldn't blame him."

He shrugged. "It's a delicate subject for a lot of people. I'm sure there are some partners who are really offended when they're asked to sign one."

"The only reason they should be offended is because they have less than pure intentions."

"Maybe."

I put my feet up on his desk and leaned back in my chair. "Guess who I saw yesterday?"

He shot a disgusted look at my shoes. "Do you mind?"

"My shoes are clean. Calm down."

"You were walking all over Manhattan in those. Bullshit, they are clean."

I rolled my eyes and put my feet back on the floor. "Simon Prescott."

"What?" he asked in shock. "When?"

"Yesterday. I got into a taxi, and he was already sitting there."

Charlie sat up in his chair and leaned forward so he could get closer to me, so he could lower his voice and I would still be able to hear. "What did he say to you?"

"That I'd made the right decision by abandoning the article. I corrected his assumption and told him I had other obligations that were more important."

"How did he even know you weren't on the story anymore?"

I shrugged. "No fucking idea. I warned Arthur about it, though. Told him not underestimate Simon."

"Is he still going to take the assignment?"

"That's what he said."

Charlie sat back in his chair and propped his chin on his closed knuckles. His gaze drifted away as he considered everything I'd just said. Then he shifted his eyes back to me. "How do you feel about it?"

"I'm not sure. I've never been this harassed by the subject of an article before."

"I was thinking the same thing."

"Normally, it would just make me go after him harder, but now that Dax and I are in this place in our lives, I realize his request wasn't unreasonable. My line of work really is dangerous, and it's smart for me to leave it behind."

He nodded. "I agree."

"I guess I feel pretty good about it. It's the first time I really feel like I have a family. Evan was just a mistake, but this is real. It's my priority now."

"That's a really mature way to look at it."

My phone vibrated in my pocket with a call, so I quickly pulled it out to make sure it wasn't important.

Charlie kept talking. "You weren't giving up anything by stepping aside. You're preparing for your future—"

"Oh my god, shut up!" I shoved my hand over his lips and silenced the words before they left his mouth. "Kat is calling me."

He pushed my arm down and leaned forward to look at my screen. "Jesus, it is her."

"What do I do?" I held up the phone to him like I had no idea how to use it.

"Just answer it."

"What if it's a butt dial?"

"You won't know unless you answer it, right?"

I finally took the call and pressed the phone to my ear. "Kat?"

After a long pause, she spoke. "Hey...can we talk?"

I sank into the chair across from her in the bar, unable to believe I was really looking at her in the flesh.

I just sat there, completely still, unable to believe she'd actually called.

She stared at me too, like she didn't know what to say. She looked down at her hands a couple times and didn't reach for her wineglass.

I could use some wine right now.

Kat glanced at my left hand where my engagement ring sat and looked back at me again. "Charlie told me that Dax proposed."

From the second I'd put the ring on, I never took it off, and I'd gotten so used to wearing it that sometimes I forgot it was there. I turned my hand over so I could look at the ring. "Yeah. I moved in last weekend."

"That's so great...happy for you."

"Thanks."

She continued to stare at me, but she didn't know what to say, where to start.

I don't know what to say either. I'd already done everything I could to repair this friendship. It was up to her to accept my apology and move on...or not move on. "Wait, you talked to Charlie?"

She nodded. "He said I'd probably want to know that you're getting married."

He didn't even tell me about it.

"This has been so hard for me, and it's just less painful if I don't see you guys anymore. When he told me you were getting married, I realized how much it would hurt if I weren't there. Not just hurt you, but hurt me too. I'm sorry that I overreacted so much...I just haven't been thinking clearly."

My eyes started to water because I finally felt at peace again, finally had my best friend back. "You didn't overreact. You're really hurt right now, and when we're hurt, we respond emotionally. It's fine."

"I know I put you in the middle, and I'm sorry for that. There really was no right answer for you, and I understand that."

"It means the world to me to hear you say that."

"You're a good person, Carson. I know you would never stab anyone in the back on purpose. I know you would never be anything less than loyal if you had the choice. It was a complicated situation."

The smart and pragmatic woman I knew was finally coming back. "We all really miss you. It'd be nice if we all got together, maybe have a game night."

"Yeah, that does sound good. I've been really lonely."

Even when I was at my happiest, I was still sad, the loss of my friend leaving a void in my heart that Dax could never fill. "I haven't been lonely, but I've been sad. Life is just not the same without you."

A half smile entered her lips.

"How about this weekend? You can come to our place and see it."

She dropped her gaze and stared at the table for a while, suddenly turning morose. "I miss all of you guys, but I still don't know how I'm gonna be able to sit there and watch the two of them be happy. Not sure if I'm ever going to be okay with it, if I'm gonna be honest."

"Charlie and Denise would never put that in your face. They'll act like friends and nothing more. We can all still hang out the way we used to, and maybe in time, when you're feeling better, things can change." I knew Charlie and Denise wouldn't mind keeping their affection nonexistent if it would make Kat more comfortable.

She gave a slight nod. "Okay. I'll try."

THE SECOND THE elevator doors opened, I sprinted into the penthouse and found Dax sitting on the couch in his sweatpants. "Oh my god, you won't believe what happened today!" I jumped onto the couch and landed on top of him, my thighs straddling his hips and my arms wrapping around his neck.

After he flinched in surprise, he released a chuckle and brought me closer. "What is it, sweetheart?"

"Kat called me! We went out for a drink and made up!"

His eyes softened like that truly made him happy. His hand squeezed me a little tighter, and a gentle smile came onto his lips. "That's really great news. I'm happy to hear that."

"I guess Charlie talked to her and told her we were getting married. She said it would make her sad if she weren't a part of my special day."

He grabbed my hands and held them together between his. "To be honest, I was getting really frustrated with her. But hearing this tells me that she's a real friend, that she loves you."

I nodded. "She does."

"How about we have her over so she can see your new place? Maybe play a game or something?"

I pulled my hands away and gave him a playful smack on the chest. "That's exactly what I was thinking. We'll all be together again—like old times."

22

DAX

I knocked on Renee's office door before I let myself inside. "You got a minute?"

Her head was bent down, and she was signing some paperwork. "What is it?" She continued to give me the cold shoulder, still palpably pissed at me.

I shut the door and approached her desk, my hands in my pockets. "Carson is going to sign a prenup. You don't have to worry about that anymore."

She steadied her pen before she lifted her chin and looked at me. "You asked her?"

I nodded. "She agreed."

The relief was unmistakable in her eyes, like my upcoming nuptials made her lose sleep at night. "I'm glad you finally came to your senses and remembered that this company is more than just yours."

"I'm doing this prenup because it's important to you. But for the record, if it were just me, I would never ask her."

She dropped her pen and leaned back in her chair as she regarded me.

"I have no doubt that we'll always be together. I have no doubt that even if it didn't work out, she wouldn't try to touch our company or our family's legacy. I fucked up with Rose, but I didn't fuck up with Carson. I'm only doing this for you, not because I don't have faith in us. I just want that to be clear."

She stared at me for a while before she said, "I never doubted your love for that woman. And if she's respectable, she won't doubt it either even though you asked her to sign it."

"She doesn't."

"Then she and I will get along just fine." She grabbed her pen again. "I'll draft up all the paperwork with our legal team, and then she'll come in and sign everything. Is that okay?"

I nodded.

"I'll let you know when it's ready."

Living with Carson was easy.

We fell into a routine immediately. My alarm clock went off before hers, and in the beginning, she used to groan in protest, but then, she just got used to it and stopped waking up every time it went off. I did my workout in my personal gym before I got ready for work.

We usually left for the office around the same time, so I had my driver drop her off on the way.

In the past, she would throw a tantrum and insist on walking, but she didn't do that at all. She just accepted it. She didn't talk about my wealth much, but she didn't make a fuss about it either. She knew it was a part of my life—plain and simple.

We never came home at the same time. Sometimes she stayed late at the office, and sometimes I did. Whenever she didn't come home, I never texted her to ask where she was. If she was no longer working on big exposés like the pharmaceutical industry, then I knew she was perfectly safe. She was either working late or getting a drink with one of her friends. And I wasn't the kind of man to keep tabs on her.

She wasn't the kind of woman who would allow it either.

She never asked where I was when I stayed at the office late. We both respected each other's independence and commitment to our jobs, which was nice. We had our time together when we were both in the penthouse, and on those crazy days, it was enough.

I loved seeing her every single night, no matter what kind of day I had. Even if we didn't say much, just having her there made me feel better. If I had to see Rose at the office, I only had to think about the woman waiting at home for me, and all my bitterness left.

Her friends claimed she was messy, but I didn't see any signs of that. She never left dishes in the sink, she didn't leave her clothes on the floor, and her vanity was always organized and tidy. Even if she weren't, it wouldn't have bothered me.

When I came home late that night, she was sitting on the couch in front of the TV with her laptop on her thighs. "Hey." She immediately perked up when she saw me, her eyes lighting up in happiness. "Guess what?"

I approached the couch then bent over to kiss her, greeting her the same way I did every day, happy to see her the moment I walked through the door.

She softened at my kiss, like she looked forward to this moment as much as I did. "I got my wedding dress."

"Yeah?"

She turned the computer around to show me what she'd picked out. "I ordered it online, and I'm going to get it fitted when it comes in."

"Thought I wasn't supposed to see the wedding dress before the big day?" I held up my hand over the screen to block it from view.

She rolled her eyes. "That's a stupid superstition. I don't buy that bullshit. We can have all the bad luck in the world and it's not going to break us, so shut up and look." She pushed my hand down so I could see the screen. "What do you think?"

It was low cut in the front and had a high slit along the leg. "Very sexy." It wasn't poufy, more of a cocktail dress, and casual. "It'll look amazing on you."

"And it'll look amazing when it's not on me too..." She waggled her eyebrows.

I chuckled then leaned down to kiss her again. "Yes." I loved it when she flirted with me, when she had the confidence to present herself as the sexy woman that she was. She wasn't arrogant about it, but not oblivious to it either.

I walked away and loosened my tie as I headed to the bedroom.

She turned back to her computer.

I went into the closet and stripped off my clothes and tossed them in the hamper so my housekeeper would take them to the dry cleaner tomorrow. I hated wearing a suit every single day. If it were up to me, I'd be in jeans and a t-shirt all the time, a hoodie in the winter months. When I turned around, I stilled when I noticed her bent over on the bed, looking back at me in just her panties.

"Fuck, I really like this living together thing." I came back to her and dropped my boxers, my cock getting hard instantly because that beautiful ass looked absolutely delicious. I kneeled at the foot of the bed and pressed my face between her cheeks, kissing that sexy pussy.

She moaned at my touch and turned her body so she could fist my hair. "Me too."

Renee came by my office. "I talked to our legal team, and everything is in order."

I was scrolling through my phone, looking at the sexy pictures Carson had sent me unexpectedly. I quickly locked the screen and turned to her. "Sorry?"

"I've got all the paperwork for Carson to sign. You think we can schedule a meeting with her tomorrow afternoon?"

"Does she need to sign this right now?" I turned in my chair to examine her.

"It's a prenup, Dax. It needs to be done before nuptials. And don't you want to get this shitty paperwork done ahead of time, that way it's not weighing on you during your actual wedding? You've only got two weeks left, and that's not even a hard date. She might wake up one day and want to do it then."

I guess that all made sense. "Fine. I'll schedule it with her."

"Good."

AFTER WORK, we met at a deli to have a dinner of sandwiches.

She had a turkey sandwich, holding it in one hand and sticking her other hand into the chip bag to grab a few before placing them in her mouth.

"Who's handling the pharma article now?" I asked as I sat across from her. I loved that we spoke to each other as good friends, just the way she did with Charlie, but we had a whole other element to our relationship that we enjoyed behind closed doors. It was a perfect balance. We had the emotional foundation, but we also wanted to fuck each other's brains out.

That was the secret to a happy relationship, if you asked me.

"My friend Arthur," she said between bites. "I warned him about Simon, so hopefully he took it seriously."

I didn't know Simon personally, but I recognized his face because I saw him at events sometimes. But now, I'd always steer clear of him—not out of fear, but because I didn't like shady people.

"Somehow, he knew I wasn't on the assignment anymore. I got into a taxi, and he was waiting for me... Creepy."

I stopped eating. "What?"

"He said I made the right decision to step down because he didn't want to kill me." She rolled her eyes. "Pompous ass. He'll get what's coming to him...eventually."

Now, I was even more grateful she'd changed departments at the paper. "Jesus fucking Christ."

"Yeah, he's a bit dramatic."

"Carson." I didn't think this was funny.

"It's over now, so it doesn't matter. I'm out of the game." She pulled her hand out of the bag and sighed.

Thank god for that. "I'm so glad you aren't doing that anymore. I couldn't get through every single day not knowing what might happen to you."

Her eyes grew serious. "Yeah. I can't risk my life anymore, not when I have someone who can't live without me."

She had no idea how true that really was. "I couldn't, sweetheart. I really couldn't." I had something money couldn't buy, and that something had made me want to live life to a new fullness.

"I had a good run and established a ruthless reputation, so I feel like I still accomplished everything I wanted."

"You're definitely ruthless." I let the serious moment pass, let us turn casual once more. It didn't make sense to stress about what could have happened when she was out of harm's way. Now, we would live a boring life together...a good life.

She continued to eat. "So, I'm thinking everyone will come over tomorrow."

"Sounds good to me."

"And I told Charlie and Denise to be as platonic as possible. I know that's not really fair to ask, but we've got to make Kat comfortable until she gets used to it. I think that's reasonable."

"She'll get desensitized to it."

"Exactly." She finished half her sandwich then moved to her second half.

I didn't want to bring up my next topic, but she already

had been receptive in the past, so it should be fine. Just get it over with. "I was wondering if you could come to the office tomorrow to sign all the paperwork."

"Paperwork for what?" she asked after she chewed her bite.

I didn't want to say it out loud. "The prenup..."

"Oh, totally forgot about that." She grabbed her phone and pulled up her calendar. "I have a thirty-minute break at two. You want to do it then?"

"That works."

"Alright, I'll be there." She set her phone down and kept eating like nothing happened.

After tomorrow afternoon, it would be over, and I wouldn't have to worry about it again. It would be in the past—and we could move on.

23

CARSON

I sat beside Charlie in his cubicle and read through his article, making marks with my pen.

Charlie sat there and watched me, his eyebrow lifting with every note I made. "That's not good."

"Well, it's not your best work."

He sighed loudly. "You're just picky."

"Being picky is what makes us good reporters. You know I'm helping you." I made another mark when my alarm went off on my phone. "Shit, I gotta go." I set the paper and pen on his desk.

"Where are you off to?" Charlie asked.

"I'm going to Dax's office to sign that prenup." I rose and wheeled my chair out of the cubicle.

"So, we're coming over later tonight?"

"Yep. And don't stick your tongue down my sister's throat."

He grinned. "I'll try."

I grabbed my bag and left the office. Dax's building wasn't too far from mine, so I could get there quickly at a brisk walk. I rose to the top floor in the elevator, and the receptionist led me to a conference room instead of his office.

When I walked inside, I stilled at the sight in front of me.

There were at least ten guys sitting there in suits. "Oh, sorry. I must be in the wrong room."

Dax stood from the table. "Sweetheart, you're in the right place."

I turned back around and took in the scene before me, all the suits with their paperwork in front of them. They all stared at me. No one greeted me. They sat at a long conference table, and on the opposite side was a single chair—for me.

I moved to the table and set my satchel down before I took a seat.

Dax sat back down.

I wasn't intimidated by anyone or anything, but I hadn't expected to step into such a hostile room, full of men I didn't even know. I thought it would be just Dax and me and a notary. But this felt like a big business deal was about to go down.

The suit next to Dax spoke. "I'm Lincoln, Mr. Frawley's lawyer. We just have some paperwork to sign. We'll get started."

One of the lawyers rose to his feet and brought me a stack of papers along with a pen.

I stilled then looked at all the papers that were obviously there for me to sign. "I have to sign all of these?" I'd assumed it would be just two pages, something I could easily look through, but there had to be thousands of pages here.

"Yes," Lincoln answered. "Mr. Frawley has a lot of assets."

I clicked the pen and pulled the paper close to me. It was a bunch of legal mumbo jumbo, and I flipped through the pages, seeing endless words that never stopped. I looked through legal briefings all the time, and this was still overwhelming.

There wasn't time to read anything, and I wasn't carrying this shit home.

I felt bulldozed.

Did I need a lawyer for this?

It was the first time I felt uncomfortable...truly uncomfortable.

I just flipped to the markers on the papers and added my signature where it was required. I didn't read a single sentence. I just finished the pile and moved it to the side and then received the next one. Like an assembly line, I made my way through one stack and received the next, and then the next...

By the end, I wanted to cry.

I felt like one of those innocent people corporations targeted, signing their life away without really understanding what they were doing. I didn't feel like a person, but like an enemy. I felt like I'd been cornered, like I was prey and they were predators.

I felt...cheap.

I didn't lift my chin to look at Dax.

I kept signing my life away, having no idea what exactly I'd signed, and just got through it.

When I stepped into the hallway to leave, Dax came after me. "Sweetheart—"

"I really have to pee. Hold on, I'll be right back."

"Okay." He slid his hands into his pockets and stood there.

I rounded the corner, moved past the bathrooms, and got the hell out of there.

When I left the building and felt the fall air hit my face, I felt a little better, but the pain in the pit of my stomach was still there...and only getting worse. I also didn't know what to do, because my home was his home—and there was nowhere else for me to go.

I didn't want to be around Dax, and I didn't know why.

I just...needed space.

I made it to the sidewalk and headed back to the office. I didn't know what else to do. I was in no mood to work, but I didn't want to go home either.

Dax called me.

I knew if I didn't answer, he would just keep calling, so I took his call. "Hey, I just got a call from my boss. I have to get back to the office right away. I'll see you later."

"Alright." There was hesitation in his voice, like he didn't believe my story but wanted to. "I'll see you at home, then."

"Okay."

"I love you." He never said that when we got off the phone. We said it rarely, so it would mean more when he spoke it aloud. But now he said it like he needed assurance that we were okay.

I said it back, but I didn't feel the way I usually did when I said it. I just said it to get him off my back, so I could take some time to figure out what had happened. "I love you too."

I HUNG out at my desk until it was time to leave.

Charlie came by my cubicle. "I'm going to go home and change. Then we'll be right over there."

"Great." I gave him a forced smile but didn't rise from my chair.

He lingered, like he saw through the façade. "Carson, you alright?"

"Oh yeah. The prime minister is being a bitch, that's all. I'll see you at my place in a bit." I almost wanted to call the whole thing off, but that would mean I'd have to explain why, and I wasn't sure how I felt at that moment.

Charlie continued to study me, but his concerns must've been assuaged because he said, "Alright. See you soon." With his satchel over his shoulder, he left the office and disappeared into the elevator.

When he was gone, I released a painful sigh. I really wished game night weren't happening tonight and we could just reschedule. But did I really need to reschedule it? I wasn't even sure what I was upset about. There was nothing wrong with signing a prenup. He had those assets before we met, and it only made sense for him to protect them. I really didn't care at all.

But that meeting didn't feel right.

It made me feel...insignificant.

I couldn't explain it. A room full of ten lawyers pushing mounds and mounds of paperwork at me? How could I possibly need to sign that many documents? Dax didn't even give me a warning about it. He didn't send me the paperwork beforehand so I could actually read what I was signing. He didn't tell me to get a lawyer, who was probably someone I should've brought with me.

I was a little guy. He was a corporation.

He crushed me.

I knew it was just business, nothing personal, but it didn't feel like an arrangement between a future husband and wife.

It felt like a demolition.

When I stepped into the penthouse, they were already there. Matt was talking to Kat, probably trying to keep her preoccupied so she wouldn't focus on Charlie and Denise.

They all turned to look at me when the elevator beeped.

"What took you so long?" Charlie asked. "What kind of host invites everybody over for game night without being here?"

Dax was in the kitchen getting the appetizers ready, and when he heard that I was in the penthouse, he stopped what he was doing and came straight to me. Now, he was in jeans and a shirt, looking like a regular person instead of the suit he'd been a few hours ago.

He stood in front of me and stared, took in the features of my face like he was afraid something had changed.

I met his look, but I didn't know what to say.

He didn't say anything either.

The gang looked back and forth at us as they picked up on the strange energy. Charlie addressed it. "Everything alright?"

I finally moved into Dax and placed a kiss on his lips. I didn't feel good doing it, just the way I didn't feel good saying I love you on the phone earlier.

His affection was muted too, like he could feel how frozen my lips were.

I took a seat on the floor in front of the armchairs. "Yeah, everything's fine. Let's get the food on the table and start the first game. What should we play?"

Dax continued to stare at me, his gaze burning into the side of my face like he didn't care that my friends were standing there watching the scene.

It was awkward for everybody because they all knew something was wrong, but they went through the motions and took seats around the coffee table.

Dax walked away and returned to the kitchen to grab appetizers to put out.

I positioned myself across from Charlie and kept my eyes down.

Dax was still out of earshot, so Charlie asked, "What's going on? Did something happen today?"

Kat leaned close and placed her hand on my arm. "Are you guys fighting?"

I saw Dax leave the kitchen and start to return to the living room. "We'll talk about it later." I grabbed the game board and set it on the table. "I know Monopoly is old, but it's a classic."

Dax sat on the floor and leaned against the couch on another side of the table. He set down his beer and placed the bowls of chips and pretzels on the surface. His eyes were on me again, boring into my face as he stared at me.

Charlie went along with what I said. "Monopoly sounds good. Let's do it."

GAME NIGHT DIDN'T HAVE its usual fun energy. We seemed to be going through the motions, but Charlie and Matt did their best to keep things moving along like there was no tension in the room.

Dax barely said two words. If he didn't know I was upset before, he definitely knew now.

As time went on, I felt worse.

I felt more uncomfortable being near him.

Dax stared at my face anytime he wasn't participating in the game, like he wanted me to know that I was the only thing on his mind right now, that there was more he wanted to say but couldn't until everybody left.

I didn't look at him at all.

I felt like I didn't know him anymore.

Charlie slid the dice toward me. "You're up, Carson."

I stared at the dice on the table without taking them. I'd officially run out of energy, pretending everything was fine. The shock of the event had worn off, and my feelings started to become clear.

They got really quiet, like they knew I was about to say something. Dax's gaze was on me with laser focus.

"I don't think I can do this." I dropped my gaze as I felt my eyes start to water. I was in pain for a lot of reasons, but the idea of losing him hurt the most.

Dax took a deep breath, just the sound alone showing all his pain. "Sweetheart, when I talked to you about the prenup, you said you were fine—"

"It's not about the prenup." I took a breath and let my wet

eyes become dry again. I lifted my chin and looked at him, my friends absolutely still like they hoped we wouldn't be able to see them if they didn't move.

His voice came out as a whisper. "Then what is it?"

I turned my head to look at him, to see the fear in his eyes. "I thought I was going to sign a two-page document that I could quickly read through. Instead, you hit me with a team of ten lawyers and notaries serving me stacks of paperwork like we were in court and you were suing me."

He sighed quietly. "My sister was in charge of all that. Since half the company is hers, she wants to make sure there's no chance that—"

"And I totally understand that. I don't care about your money. I don't want it. But I just…felt so insignificant. I felt like a weak person facing off against a corporation I couldn't possibly beat. It was dirty, the way the paperwork was served to me without me even having an opportunity to read it or understand what I was signing. Prenups are ten pages at most, Dax. Why did I need to sign two-thousand-pages' worth of paperwork?"

Everyone's eyes shifted back and forth as they watched us talk.

Dax was quiet as he considered his answer. "Because the corporation owns a lot of different assets in all different facets—"

"Why didn't you explain that to me? Why weren't there just two pieces of paper that said everything that's yours remains yours? Why did you let me walk in there and look like an idiot while I was ganged up on by a bunch of suits?"

"You weren't ganged up on—"

"This was supposed to be between you and me, husband and wife, along with a lawyer and a couple pieces of paper. This didn't feel intimate at all. This was a sterile conquering. You didn't even tell me to bring my lawyer."

"I didn't know it would be that extensive—"

"Or you didn't want me to have a chance to even look at anything. Dax, I live in the world of corporate greed, and I know exactly how these situations play out. I have less power than you, so you abused your power over me to get everything you wanted without even bothering to explain what I was signing. You took advantage of me."

He shook his head, his eyes becoming more distressed. "It wasn't like that."

"It was *exactly* like that," I snapped. "We both know I couldn't care less about your money, that I love you despite your wealth, not because of it. I wasn't offended when you asked me to sign it because it's nothing personal. But this behavior indicates that you don't trust me at all, that you want me to sign my life away without even giving me any transparency at all." I couldn't sit still anymore, and I got to my feet because I needed to move; I needed to step away so everyone wasn't so close to me.

Dax was on his feet quickly, then came after me. "Let's just forget the prenup, alright? I'll have it voided tomorrow."

"It was never about the prenup, and you know that."

"Well, here's me being transparent. Here's me shredding all of that to be with you. Even if you took all my money someday, it would still be worth it to be with you now. So let's just forget it—"

"I've lived in this world since I graduated college, and being in that environment just reminds me why I hate it so much. Money is the root of all evil, and look what it did to us."

He stood in front of me with his hands squeezed tightly into fists, a terrified look in his eyes. "It's done nothing to us. I'm sorry how that was handled, but Renee is pulling the strings here—not me."

"I'm not marrying Renee. I'm marrying *you*. Why is she the one orchestrating all this?" I raised my voice as I became angrier. "Why were you sitting across the table from me instead of beside me? Don't you see what happened? We were enemies."

He shook his head. "That's not what happened."

"That was exactly what happened. I don't want to live in this world. I don't want to be married to a man who lives his life this way. Who serves his fiancée mounds of paperwork like that? What did you even have me sign?"

He came closer to me. "Look, that was Renee protecting her assets. It doesn't have anything to do with us."

"You could've met with me first and told me everything in those documents, and I would've believed you. You could have outlined what happens in the event you die and I survive you. You could've told me how our wealth would be handed down to our children, if I would be entitled to your life insurance if you got hit by a bus, but I don't know any of that because it's buried in a mountain of paperwork. There was no conversation. Not a single word."

"Alright." He breathed hard like he'd just run a mile, wore a look full of despair, like he didn't know how to handle this situation. "Let's start over. We'll go through everything together—"

"You shouldn't have to do that just because I requested it. You should've done that in the first place. Didn't you think we should talk about this? No. You completely took control and didn't think I was important enough to be part of the conversation."

"I'm telling you, it wasn't like that. I wouldn't even have asked you to sign anything if Renee didn't make me." All the veins in his arm started to pop, along with the ones in his neck. He threw his arms down in ferocity. "Don't let this divide us. You know I love you and trust you. I'll resign from the company and sign over all my shares to my sister tomorrow, and we can go live in a regular apartment with regular lives. Nothing is more important to me in this world than you."

I dropped my chin, my eyes becoming moist once again.

"Sweetheart, please."

My hands moved to my hips, and I closed my eyes, feeling the tears drip down my cheeks. "This is always going to be a problem, isn't it?"

He was quiet.

"You lied about who you were because you didn't trust me to know that you were a billionaire. Now, you're having all these clandestine meetings behind my back and shoving mountains of paperwork at me that you expect me to sign with no questions asked. You constantly expect me to trust you, but you never trust me." I lifted my gaze and stared at him, no longer fighting the tears that couldn't be stopped.

"You are the person I trust most in this world—"

"Well, you don't show it very well," I snapped. "You asked me to give up my job for you. I've made compromises for this relationship, really big compromises, and then you do me dirty like that."

"I didn't do you dirty—"

"I'm tired of being in a relationship where I'm always getting the short end of the stick. I'm tired of feeling like the one at the mercy of your power."

His face began to flush, and a moist sheen covered his eyes.

"I'm tired of this relationship being complicated because of who you are. I forgave your lie and moved on because I love you, but this is always going to come between us. Even if we get married and move forward, this situation is always gonna pop back up."

"No. What's mine is yours—"

"No, it's not. What happens if you die? Do I inherit your ownership of the company? Or does it go back to your sister? What about if we have kids? The fact that I don't know any of this and you expect me to sign off like I do is a slap in the face."

He stood there in silence as he struggled to find a response. Everything was happening so fast, and he had an entire audience there to watch the scene unfold. "We have established that I haven't handled this well. I'm telling you, Renee was pulling the strings of this whole thing. Let's go back to the office tomorrow and start over."

He didn't get it. "It shouldn't be this hard to be with somebody."

His eyes started to fall when he understood where this conversation was headed.

"It shouldn't be this complicated."

"Don't say that."

"It's just not meant to be..." There was no doubt that I loved him. I loved him so much, but this relationship had been a roller coaster since the beginning. "Our relationship started on a lie, and then when we got here, you start our marriage with deception. It doesn't feel right anymore."

Dax was absolutely still, his eyes wide with disbelief. He continued to breathe through the pain that weighed down his shoulders and brought him flat against the earth. Our eye contact seemed to be too painful for him because he dropped his gaze and ran his hand across his jawline.

When I'd woken up that morning, the sky was blue and it was a beautiful day. The leaves in Central Park were turning brown and red as the season deepened. But once I stepped into that office, everything changed.

"Sweetheart..." He raised his gaze to look at me again, his eyes reflected the light of the lamp behind me. "Don't do this. I didn't even want a prenup in the first place. I don't want it, not because I'm an idiot who doesn't learn from my mistakes, but because I have absolute faith that we will be together forever. I said those words to my sister, but they weren't enough to make her feel better. Yes, all that paperwork was a corporate stunt, but I had nothing to do with it. And I don't even know all the details of that prenup because I really don't care what it says."

I stepped back because everything had shattered for me already. This penthouse didn't feel like my home. This man didn't feel like my fiancé. I'd spent a lot of my time trying to make this work, and the truth was, it was never meant to be. "This is why rich people only marry rich people. It's much easier that way."

He shook his head. "We belong together. You know that."

"If we belong together, it shouldn't be this hard. We've been trying to make it work and have never been successful."

"Well, this time, we will be successful," he said firmly.

"I don't feel the same way anymore, Dax." I couldn't look at him. The moment was too painful to experience in the present, so I pulled away to protect both my heart and mind.

It was quiet for a long time.

My arms crossed over my chest, and I stepped farther away. All my stuff was there because it was my home, but I suddenly felt like it wasn't my home at all. I couldn't stay there another night. "I should go."

Dax didn't fight for me, either because he didn't want to or because it wouldn't make a difference. He backed away and gave me space.

Charlie and everyone else got up from the floor. They came toward me so they could walk me out. Charlie hit the button for the elevator; Kat placed her hand on my arm.

Like it was too hard to watch me, Dax turned around completely and left the living room. He moved to the dining table where there was a view of the city and took a seat. His shoulders sank with weakness. His eyes stared out the window and never looked back at me.

I'd forgotten about the ring on my left hand because it had felt right from the moment I put it on, like it was a part of my skin at this point. But I pulled it off my left hand and set it on the coffee table next to the game board and bowl of chips.

I turned away and stepped into the elevator with my friends. I stood in the middle and faced Dax, looking at him for the last time.

Charlie placed his hand on my arm, telling me he was there.

The doors closed.

And that was it.

We were over.

24

CARSON

My bedroom furniture was still in the apartment, so I went to sleep like nothing had changed.

Charlie sat with me for a while at the end of the bed, but he didn't try to engage in a lengthy conversation, knowing I just wanted to lie there in silence.

When he left and turned off the light, I went straight to sleep.

Like I had no energy.

When I woke up the next day, I moved like a zombie. I threw my clothes in the dryer to de-wrinkle them and put them back on so I could wear them to the office.

If anyone noticed I was wearing the same clothes as yesterday, they probably wouldn't say anything.

And if they did, I'd tell them to fuck off.

I made myself a mug of coffee at the kitchen counter and took a drink, my eyes still puffy from crying the night before.

Charlie made scrambled eggs on the stove and dished them onto a plate before he handed it to me.

"I'm not hungry."

Charlie turned off the stove and made a plate for himself. "You're still going to the office today?"

"Yeah." I stared out the window over the sink and looked at the city outside.

"You have a lot of sick days built up. You don't want to use one?"

"No."

He pulled out a fork from the drawer and dug it into his eggs so he could take a bite.

"Is it okay if I move back in?"

His chewing slowed, and he looked at me incredulously, like it was a stupid question. "Always."

I took another drink from my mug and then poured it into the sink because I had to get going.

"But are you sure about this?"

I nodded. "If a relationship is hard now, it won't get easier. I've been divorced once. I'm not going to do it again."

Charlie continued to stare at me, not giving his two cents on the matter. "All right."

"Relationships aren't always easy. Sometimes they take hard work. It's not always butterflies in your stomach kind of happiness. But I feel like Dax and I have been overrun with problems since the moment we met, and all those problems come from his billionaire status. Money makes things complicated. I just don't need anything more complicated in my life."

He nodded.

"Instead of just being in love, we'll always be dictated by his money. He had no idea how shitty it felt to walk into his conference room and have those suits staring at me like I was the enemy."

"Yeah. It was pretty shitty."

"I thought it would just be Dax and a lawyer, and we would just go over the paperwork. Casual. Transparent. But I walked in there, and it was really clear I wasn't entitled to information about my own marriage. I was in no place to negotiate, and they knew that. So, it was either sign it…or we don't trust you. It is not a good way to start a marriage."

He agreed. "No, it's not." He set his plate and fork down like he'd lost his appetite because of our conversation. "I think Dax is a good guy, and he has nothing but good intentions. But when you marry somebody, you don't just marry them but everything they're associated with. So that's the kind of life you'll have to live, with someone who is guarded about their wealth, where their money is a liability more than an asset."

"Exactly."

"And you'll always be an outsider because of it. I wonder if he passed away if you would get anything at all or if everything would go to Renee or your children. Are you always prohibited from gaining any of his assets? Those are really important questions to ask, and it's unacceptable that this wasn't a conversation prior to your being asked to sign the contracts."

I'd really expected Charlie to try to talk me into going back to Dax, and it was a relief that he saw my point of view. As journalists, we had to deal with rich people all the time, write articles about their wealth and inheritances. We understood exactly how these things worked. I knew what I'd signed up for with Dax, but I didn't expect him to go about it in such a disrespectful way. "Thanks."

He sighed deeply and crossed his arms over his chest. "Want to watch a movie after work? We can order pizza or something."

I smiled at the offer. "You don't have to hang out with me, Charlie. I'm sure you're eager to spend time with Denise since you just got together."

"Bros before hoes, right?"

I chuckled. "There're a lot of offensive things in that sentence."

"Why do you think I said it?" He grabbed his mug and took another drink before he poured it out in the sink.

"Why don't you invite her over too? I don't mind hanging out with both of you."

"You're sure?"

"Of course. She's my sister. Just don't have obnoxiously loud sex after work."

He gave me a thumbs-up. "You got it."

I knocked on his open door before I stepped inside his office. "Can I talk to you for a second?"

Vince looked up from his phone and set it down on his desk. "What's up?"

"My life plans have changed. Can I get the Simon Prescott article back?"

He turned slightly in his chair as he stared at me. "Everything alright?"

"My fiancé and I broke up. So, not really." I fell into the armchair in front of his desk and kept a stoic expression, brushing off the news like it didn't affect me as much as it really did. "But it will be alright...eventually."

Vince stared at me through his glasses, taking his time before he found a response. "I'm sorry to hear that, Carson. You seemed happy."

"Well, happiness is only temporary...just as sadness is."

"Ordinarily, I would say no to your request, but Arthur just dropped the article, and I don't have the time to bring someone else up to speed. It's yours."

My eyebrow cocked. "Why'd he drop the article?"

"His dad had a stroke back in Ohio. Needs to take medical leave."

"Oh, that's terrible."

"Yeah," he said with a shrug. "So, get back on it. And try to hustle. We've lost a lot of time switching hands so many times."

Kat sat across from me in the bar, her finger on the straw that extended out of her fruity drink. "I'm sorry, girl."

"I know." I sat with my elbows on the table and my eyes on the surface, my hands digging into my hair. "I'm just happy that you're here with me, that we're talking about boys the way we used to."

The corner of her mouth rose in a slight smile. "There's the silver lining."

"I got my article back."

"The one Dax asked you to give up?"

I nodded. "I changed my career plans for him, and now that he's gone, I'm going back to my old life. It's ironic that he asked me to give up my dream, then served me a bunch of paperwork that required me to give up god knows what."

"Yeah, it's rough. But are you sure this is what you want?"

"What I want?" I asked in surprise. "No, I don't want to lose Dax. I loved that man. I couldn't sleep last night because he wasn't there, and I'm used to him being there. But if a relationship isn't right in the beginning, it's not going to be right later. I should have just stayed away after he lied."

"Maybe..."

Every relationship I had seemed to be a huge mistake. That was why I'd now decided to stay away from relationships altogether. The high wasn't worth the fall—not by a long shot.

"Has he tried to talk to you?"

I shook my head. "He knows it's over." Even if he was innocent in the whole thing, he knew his world was so different from mine that it would always divide us. He could never really let me in because of everything that had happened, and I wouldn't let him in ever again.

"Maybe we should just get together and be done with it."

I raised my glass from the table. "I'll drink to that."

25

DAX

It was an out-of-body experience.

I was so devastated that I didn't know how to behave.

Everything unfolded in front of my eyes, getting worse and worse, as I watched her pull away more and more. It was like a horror film, losing the love of my life. And when the ending finally arrived, I knew there was nothing I could do to stop it.

So I let her go.

There would always be obstacles between us because of my wealth. There would always be a fine line between us—my family's wealth and then her. I would always have one foot on each side of the line, unable to fully give myself to a single person.

It sucked.

I didn't go to work the next day. I kept up with things through my laptop but never got out of my pajamas. I didn't shower or brush my teeth.

Whatever.

By the end of the day, Renee texted me. *Everything okay?*

Just had stuff to do at home today.

Are you sure? Because you never don't come in.

I said I'm fine. I resented my sister because she was

responsible for all of this, but I also didn't blame her. She was just protecting her own interests, which were unfortunately attached to the decisions I'd made. *I'll see you later.*

I sat at the table and looked out the window, watching the sun fade and darkness spread over the city. I had nowhere to go. I had no purpose. Carson had been the most important person in my life, and she'd just walked away.

I didn't go after her because it was pointless.

There was no hope this time.

She was right. It was too complicated, and I didn't handle everything well. I should have been more involved instead of letting my sister take charge. The only reason I was so clinical about the whole thing was because I didn't want to be involved at all. The assets didn't matter to me. But from Carson's point of view, it did look like an attack.

It did look like she didn't matter.

I grabbed my phone again and texted Charlie. *How is she?*

The three dots came and went, like he wrote a message, deleted it, wrote it again, went back and forth because he didn't know what to do. *I'm sorry it didn't work out between you guys because you were great together, but I'm Carson's best friend and I don't think we should talk anymore. Take care, man.*

I got dumped again, this time by her friends, and that hurt just as much.

Because they had become my friends.

My family.

The next few days were lifeless.

I went to work but didn't give a damn about what I was doing.

The company could burn to the ground for all I cared.

The idea of having to go out and meet someone new at

some point sounded like torture. I'd already found exactly what I wanted for the rest of my life, and I didn't want to move on. I didn't want to lose that. I just wanted it back.

I went to work then went home, scrounging for food in the fridge instead of cooking like I usually did. Scotch became my best friend.

My only friend.

My phone lit up with a text from Charlie. *I'm outside your building. Do you mind if I come up and grab her stuff?*

Living with her shit was the worst part. Her clothes were still on the floor, and I didn't touch them. Her beauty products were still on the counter in my bathroom. I wanted them to disappear so I could go back to my lonely existence, but the idea of her stuff being gone forever seemed like another version of goodbye. *Sure.*

Be up in a sec.

I stayed on the couch in my sweatpants, rocking a full beard because I'd stopped shaving. The game was on, and my glass of scotch was never empty, no matter how much I drank.

Minutes later, the elevator beeped, the doors opened, and Charlie stepped into the living room. He took a quick scan then settled his gaze on me. For a brief moment, he wore a look of pity, like he could see my struggle in just a simple look.

I dragged my hands down my face before I stood up. "Need help?"

"Matt has the van downstairs."

"Is she with you?"

He shook his head.

"Then I'll help you."

Charlie didn't decline the offer, and together, we went into my bedroom and placed her clothes into boxes. We worked in silence, packing up her entire essence like she'd never been there in the first place.

I finished one box and set it on the edge of my bed. "How is she?"

Charlie dropped her beauty products into a box, and they thudded when they hit the hard surface below. "She's fine."

"Fine like me, or actually fine?"

He shrugged. "It's a tie."

At least I wasn't alone in my sorrow.

She'd left her engagement ring on my coffee table, and I hadn't touched it. What the hell was I supposed to do with it? Put it in my nightstand? Every time I looked at it, it would just hurt. I wanted her to take it back, because it was a gift that showed my love, which was eternal. But she never would. "You think there's any chance for us?"

He lifted the box then carried it to the edge of the bed, rarely making eye contact with me, like he wanted to keep me at a physical and emotional distance. "No."

"Look, my sister was the one in charge of all that—"

"I'm not part of this, Dax. She made her decision, and I understand why she made that decision."

Her best friend wasn't on my side, and now I really had no chance. "But I went to you first and asked for your advice. You know I never wanted to do that prenup in the first place. You know that."

"Yes, I do know that."

"Then tell her," I snapped.

He picked up the box but then decided to put it back down because this conversation couldn't be prevented. "Everything that happened before and after that meeting is moot. She walked into a room with a shit-ton of lawyers and got her ass handed to her. That was how *you* decided to start that marriage. That's the dividing line."

I shook my head. "That's not how I decided to start it, okay? I didn't want it to be that way."

"Blame it on your sister all you want, but all you had to do was move to the other side of that table. But you didn't. You act like that money means nothing to you, but you're full of shit. You know you are."

"I'm not full of shit. The money has brought me nothing but misery and only made me lonely. What I do care about is my family's legacy, for the work and dedication of my father and his father. If I didn't try to protect that, what kind of man would I be? It's easy for you guys to see it the way you do because you have no idea what it's like."

He picked up the box then gave me a long, cold stare. "And you have no idea what it's like to be sitting across that table, to be pushed around because you only have a few dollars to your name." He turned to walk out. "To be treated like shit by yet another rich person..."

I watched him go and felt the concrete slab land in my stomach.

Charlie carried the boxes outside then returned a few minutes later.

I had the ring in my hand and extended it to him. "Give this back to her."

He eyed it but didn't take it. "She gave it back to you because she doesn't want it."

"It was a gift. She can sell it if she wants—"

"Trust me, she wants nothing to do with it." He turned away and kept walking.

I squeezed the ring in my fist as I sighed deeply. Then I opened a random drawer in the kitchen I never used and dropped it inside since I would hardly ever see it there. Then I grabbed another box and helped Charlie carry it downstairs, where Matt was organizing things in the back.

Matt stilled when he saw me. "Hey, Dax." He hopped out of the van and landed on the sidewalk.

"Hey, man." We didn't greet each other with a handshake like we used to. "How are you?"

He shrugged. "Times are weird right now."

Charlie walked back inside to get more boxes, like he wanted to get this over with as soon as possible.

I thought I might get more information out of Matt. "How is she?"

He slid his hands into his front pockets and gave a shrug. "You know, throwing herself back into work like usual."

I knew exactly how she was, choosing to mask her pain by working crazy hours and hooking up with random guys. I tried not to think about it. Otherwise, I would never get out of bed again. "She's taking on more assignments?"

"She asked for her old job back, actually."

My heart stopped beating—literally.

Matt rubbed the back of his neck then looked at the door, waiting for Charlie to come back.

I was even more horrified than I was before. The breakup was hard enough to handle, but knowing she put herself back into the line of fire was sickening. The thought hadn't even crossed my mind. I thought once she stepped down, someone else filled that spot and she wouldn't be able to go backward.

Matt studied me for a bit, like he knew the blood was draining from all my extremities. "You okay, man?"

"No...I'm not."

"You've been avoiding me all week." Renee walked into my office even though my assistant tried to prevent her from stepping into my space. "What is your deal?"

Since the damage had been done, my assistant gave up.

Renee walked across the large room, her heels tapping against the hardwood. "Dax?"

I stared at her coldly, putting all the blame for my failed relationship on her shoulders. "Carson left me."

She stilled at the edge of my desk, sincere pain moving into her eyes. "What happened?"

"What happened?" I said it with a slight chuckle, a dark tone that defied my laughter. I rose to my feet because I couldn't sit anymore. "She came in to sign a prenup but ended up in the court of law. Were two thousand papers really necessary?"

"It's a big company—"

"It was totally unnecessary. Carson told me she had no problem signing away her rights to everything—because she loved me and not my wallet. And now she's gone—because we treated her like shit. The only woman who's ever loved me for me is gone—because of you." I'd never been so furious with my sister, never regarded with this level of disgust.

Speechless, Renee just stared at me.

I released a loud sigh then fell into my chair again. "Now, she's back at her old position—which is probably going to get her killed. She moved her shit out of my penthouse, so I'm alone. She's probably spending her nights doing god knows what while I stare at the ceiling all fucking night. We were never going to get a divorce anyway, so this was all fucking stupid. I lost her before I even had her. But thank god I have all our money..."

"Rose—"

"She's not Rose." My voice grew so loud, so quickly, making the walls vibrate. "No fucking comparison. Rose was a stupid mistake that I'll always have to regret, but Carson was the one. I'll never find another woman like that, so you've damned me to an eternity of fucking hell."

Renee dropped her chin again. "Let me talk to her—"

"Don't go anywhere near her, Renee. It's done. You opening your stupid fucking mouth isn't going to fix a goddamn thing." My rage skyrocketed, and I knocked everything off my desk, my laptop smashing on the floor, the vase shattering into pieces. I got to my feet then turned to the window, unable to look at her stupid face for a moment longer. "Get the fuck out."

I STEPPED into the office at the *New York Press* and walked across the floor to the editor's office. My eyes scanned for Carson, but she wasn't there.

But Charlie was.

He looked up from his desk, his confused eyes following me across the floor as I approached Vince's office.

I knocked on the door before I let myself inside.

Vince was on the phone. "Yes, I'll get someone on it. We'll talk later." He hung up then turned his gaze on me. "Who the fuck are you?"

I approached his desk with the check in my hand. I set it on the surface in front of him. "That's all yours—if you do something for me."

He looked down at the million-dollar check—made out to cash—and then lifted his gaze to look at me.

"Keep Carson off the dangerous stuff, and that's yours."

Without looking at it again, he pushed the check back across the desk to me. "If you think people haven't tried to buy me off before, you obviously know nothing about the newspaper business. And frankly, I've been offered a lot more to do a lot less. Your money doesn't impress me. We're the most respected paper in the country because we care about the truth. Integrity, honesty, hard work, those are the values that matter to us—not money. Pay off your executives and your other corporate sleazebags. That shit doesn't work here. You may be richer than us, but you aren't better than us. Carson is one of my top journalists, and if she wants to risk her neck to secure the truth, that's her choice. Now, you can take that check and shove it up your ass—asshole."

I held his gaze, frustrated that I didn't get my way, but I was forced to respect him. He reminded me of Carson, who was dedicated to being honest and transparent. I took the check back and turned away. "Thank you for your time." I stepped out of his office and walked back to the elevators.

Charlie came to my side. "What the hell are you doing?"

"Nothing." I didn't look at him and kept walking.

"Fucking answer me." He grabbed me by the arm and halted my movement.

I turned to him as I folded the check and slipped it into my pocket. "Nothing. Vince didn't go for it."

"Go for what?"

"I tried to pay him to keep Carson on less high-profile articles."

His eyes narrowed. "You think that shit is going to work on the most respected editor in the industry?"

I'd learned my lesson the hard way. "I respect what you do here. I just don't want Carson to get hurt." I would always want to keep her safe, always have her back when she thought I wasn't looking.

"No offense, but she's not your problem anymore. It's pretty fucked up that you would try to interfere with her job like that."

"You know what else is fucked up?" I countered. "That you let your best friend risk her life when her life is far more valuable than a fucking article." I tried to keep my voice low so the other reporters wouldn't turn to watch us. "How can you just let her stick her neck out like that? How can you just look the other way?"

His nostrils flared as he breathed hard. "It's what she wants."

"But it's not what's best for her. She takes on these stories because she has nothing else to live for. Don't you understand that? She doesn't have a husband or kids, so she sees her life as expendable. She's too scared to give herself to somebody, so she does this, which is less scary to her."

"And you can blame yourself for that." He cast me one last glare before he turned his back and walked away.

Charlie and Vince would both tell Carson what I tried to do.

She'd be pissed.

I didn't care. I'd do it again.

Days passed, and I spent my time alone in my penthouse. I'd hoped my stunt would cause her to call and scream at me, but she never did. Even if she were spewing hate, it would still be nice to hear her voice, no matter how angry she was.

But nothing happened.

I was in my office when my sister stopped by for another visit.

It was hard for me to look at her and not be furious. I needed to take responsibility for the way I'd handled things, but she was the root of the problem. She'd always been difficult with Carson because she didn't trust anyone—even though I was the one who was humiliated by Rose.

I stared her down as she walked to my desk with a folder of paperwork.

She set the folder on my desk and slid it toward me. "I have an idea that might help you."

I didn't open the folder. "Help with what?"

"Carson."

Nothing would help me with her at this point.

When I didn't open the folder, she bent down and did it for me. "Sign all your shares over to me."

I cocked an eyebrow.

"Give me full ownership of the company. So, in the event of a divorce, there's nothing to worry about. You don't need to have her sign anything, because all your other assets are yours personally."

I glanced at the paper before I looked up at her again. "Look how that worked out."

"Dax, come on. That's not how it is. You know I'll give you back your shares in a heartbeat. Nothing here has to change. We'll keep everything exactly the same. But you can do this to protect your family's company, and it eliminates the problem altogether."

"Little late." Should have done this is in the first place.

"Talk to her again and see if this changes things. You're protecting your family's company, but everything else that belongs to you is on the table and you aren't asking her to sign anything—to prove that you have complete faith in your relationship. It's romantic. Stupid, but romantic."

I looked at the paper again and pulled it closer to me. I scanned through a few lines before I grabbed a pen, clicked it, and signed my name. "I guess it's worth a try."

26

CARSON

"I can't believe he did that." I sat on the couch in front of the TV, while Charlie sat on the armchair, Denise on the floor between his legs with her back against the chair.

Charlie shook his head. "I can."

Dax was stupid to think that a fat check would manipulate the people in my office. We'd been threatened by terrorist groups with bombs, and we didn't blink an eye. "Idiot."

"It's kind of romantic," Denise said. "He's still trying to protect you."

"I don't need him to protect me." My eyes turned back to the TV to watch the game, my beer between my thighs.

Matt knocked on the door.

Without turning to look, I called out, "It's open."

After a pause, the door opened.

Charlie turned to greet Matt, but he turned white in the face instead.

I turned to see for myself.

It wasn't Matt. It was Dax. He was in jeans and a long-sleeved shirt, thick hair over his jawline because he wasn't shaving as religiously as he used to. A permanent look of sadness was in his eyes, and the look intensified the longer he looked at me. He pushed the door shut behind him.

"We thought you were Matt." I set the beer on the table and rose to my feet to face him. "So, the invitation is revoked."

His hands slid into his front pockets like he intended to stick around.

"Did you hear what I said?" I snapped.

"Will you hear what I have to say?" he asked calmly.

"Why would I?" I walked around the couch so I could get closer to him, to chase him out of the apartment. "Dax, it's over. Don't come to my office and try to pay off my editor. He's had a gun to his head, and he didn't even blink. You have no idea who you're up against. Your flimsy piece of paper is nothing to people like us. We don't throw money around to solve our problems. We fight—"

He held up his hand to silence me. "I won't apologize for what I did. I'm just trying to keep you safe. When Matt told me you went back to your old position, it scared me." He slowly lowered his hand, his voice still gentle despite the rage in mine. "Because I love you like you're still my fiancée, and there will never be a time in the future when I don't love you that way, even if you're married to somebody else. Carson, I know I fucked up—"

I crossed my arms over my chest and took a step back. "Please don't make this harder than it needs to be." It was easier to be angry at his actions, so when he took that away and I was just sad, it was unbearable. I missed him every morning and every night. My apartment didn't even feel like home anymore...because he was home.

"It doesn't have to be hard at all," he whispered, his eyes emotional as he stared at me. "I'm sorry for the way I handled everything. Truly, I am. I have a solution to that problem, what I should have done in the first place, what I wanted to do before Renee sabotaged my intentions."

I dropped my gaze to the floor. "It's not going to make a difference. What's done is done."

"I think we're worth more than that, Carson."

I was forced to lift my chin and look at him again.

He stared at me for a long time, like all he wanted was to look at my face. It somehow comforted him rather than reminded him of the distance between our hearts. "Look, I signed over all my shares of the company to my sister. So, she retains complete ownership—minus Rose's shares. Now I don't need you to sign anything at all, because all my personal assets are mine to do with whatever I want. You can even ask Charlie, I never wanted to ask you to sign anything in the first place because I have complete faith that we're going to last forever. I don't need a prenup, and even if you wanted to get one, my answer would still be no. Let's try this again." He inhaled a deep breath and slowly let it out. "Please."

My arms tightened across my chest, and I turned my gaze away, because it was too hard to look at him and think clearly. "I don't—"

"Don't throw us away because of that shitshow, alright?" He turned more aggressive, attacking the second he spotted my hesitation, when he knew there was hope this could work. "I handled it poorly, and I apologize for that. But this is my new offer, what I wanted to do in the first place. I'm just sorry I didn't think of it sooner."

My hands rubbed up and down my arms just so I could fidget.

"Sweetheart..."

I tried to even out my breathing, but I still didn't look at him. This time apart had made me miss him more, not less. I didn't resume my old life and brush off the breakup like it never happened. The pain was always in my chest; it was always terrible. All my stuff was back in the apartment, but that bedroom felt foreign now. "I don't know..."

He inhaled a deep breath. "Look at me."

I finally turned back to him.

"This is too damn good to throw away, alright? It's worth it. It is." He raised his hands slightly and tightened them into fists, his knuckles turning white because he was so anxious to get the answer he wanted.

"I gave up my job once, and I won't do it again." I wasn't going to go back into Vince's office and change my mind for a second time. I'd look like a fucking idiot if I did. "I already humiliated myself once to my boss, and luckily he still respects me, so I'm not going to squander his good opinion for you once more. I'm willing…if you make this compromise."

His hands immediately slackened, and his skin started to grow more and more pale, like the terror was turning his skin white everywhere. His eyes were open and frozen, like he hadn't anticipated that counter. "You were going to give it up anyway—"

"Nonnegotiable."

He inhaled another deep breath.

"If you do this again, these are my terms. I already sacrificed my job for you once. I already forgave you for all the lies you spewed. I already left my apartment and moved in to your place. I already agreed to sign everything you wanted me to sign. I'm the only one making compromises here, and I'm done with that."

Now, he was the one that looked away. "What about kids?"

"We can still do that."

"If someone wants to target you, they're going to target your family. I can live with that to be with you because my life is mine to gamble. But I won't risk my children. I won't. Here's another compromise—you keep your job until we have a family. Then you walk away."

I shook my head. "No."

The life left his eyes.

"I shouldn't have to choose between being a mother and having a career—"

"You know the career has nothing to do with it. It's the danger associated with your job."

I didn't want to be obligated to do something sometime in the future when I had no idea how I might feel about it at that point. "You have a lot of money to keep us safe—"

"Still not worth the risk. Come on, Carson—"

"No. Take it or leave it."

His arms slowly dropped to his sides, and now he looked devastated, like he was losing me all over again. "I will make any compromise you want to make this work. I will walk away from my job altogether, give all my money to charity, whatever you want. But your job puts your life at risk every fucking day, and I can't live that way—never knowing if you're going to come home."

"Police officers and firefighters do it every day—"

"Their jobs aren't nearly as dangerous as yours, and you know it." He dug his fingers into his hair for a moment, fisting it hard in frustration. "Carson, please..."

"No. That's my final answer. Take it or leave it."

The energy quickly changed, taking a nose dive, plummeting hard until it hit the ground with a collision that shook the earth. He looked away, appearing lifeless, empty, full of despair. Seconds passed before he turned back to look at me. "You know I can't take that." He shifted his gaze back to me. "I know I've fucked up a lot, but my intentions were always good and my situation made it difficult to see that. But I'm not asking for anything unreasonable. You know I'm not. The only reason you aren't giving it to me is because it's an excuse, because you're scared to do this again, and you'd rather take the comfort of your job and the reputation it gives you. You'll either die because of it, or you'll live long enough to be replaced by somebody better. If you're willing to choose that over love, over having a family, over me...then maybe you never really loved me in the first place."

He gave me a disappointed look, as if his opinion of me had changed. "I've had to put up with a lot of shit from you too. You treated me like an object rather than a person when I wanted to actually connect with you. I've always accepted your headstrong attitude and your independence, when other men would be intimidated or simply annoyed. Instead of focusing on my flaws, you should focus on all the good things I've done for you and this relationship. I'm a pretty good guy, and you aren't going to find anyone better than me out there. So, if you're going to throw this away because of a huge misunderstanding, because I was trying to do right by my family after my first mistake, then maybe this isn't right. Maybe it is best if we call it quits and go our separate ways. You aren't the only one tired of making compromises. All I've ever wanted was to love you, and you made it a fucking pain in the ass every step of the way."

Now, he was furious as well as disappointed, like his heart stopped loving me within a few beats. He gave me a final look before he turned around and left the apartment.

I stood there and stared at the door, my arms still crossed over my chest, my breathing getting shallower and harder with every second that passed. My eyes glistened and turned wet, and my chest wanted to heave with the approaching sobs.

The door opened again, and Matt stepped inside. "What happened? I just saw Dax in the hallway looking like he was going to demolish this building when he gets downstairs..." He stilled when he saw the look on my face.

I burst into tears—and I couldn't keep it in any longer.

I SAT at my desk and typed on my computer, finishing my notes on the prime minister before sending it off to Abby, the reporter who would take over the position.

Charlie stepped into my cubicle and placed a sandwich next to my laptop. "Just got lunch. Thought you might be hungry."

I gave a slight smile as I looked at it. "You don't have to buy me lunch every day, Charlie."

"I thought I would grab something while I was out." He took a seat and unwrapped his sandwich so he could eat it beside me.

I turned back to my computer like he wasn't even there. My final conversation with Dax had been a few days ago, and none of my friends had asked me about it, as if they were giving me time to decompress without an interrogation.

He took a few bites and looked at my notes. "How are things with Simon Prescott?"

"I'm meeting a source tonight. I just need a couple more details confirmed, and then I'll submit it to Vince."

He kept eating, pulling the wrapper farther away to reveal more of the sandwich. "How are you?"

"Fine."

"You sure?"

My fingers stopped on the keyboard, and I released a sigh. "Yes."

"You don't look fine."

"Well, I am."

Charlie stopped eating his sandwich and set it down. "You're sadder now than you were before."

"Well, breakups do that to you. The pain comes at different times."

He moved his hand to my laptop and closed it. "Carson."

"We're really going to do this now? At work?" I turned to look at him.

"I've been waiting for you to do it on your own time, but

it's obvious that's not going to happen." He studied my face like he was trying to read my real feelings through my features rather than through the words I chose. "I've been thinking about what Dax said...and I think he's right. I also think you think it too—and that's why you're so sad."

I dropped my gaze because eye contact was too much. "I thought you didn't like him after what he did."

"Never said that. I don't dislike him. I just...didn't agree with how he handled the situation."

"But nothing has changed."

"Exactly," he said. "You still love each other. And his solution is a great declaration. He's putting everything on the table to prove to you that he's not sleazy. When we talked, he told me he didn't even want you to sign anything in the first place, as a gesture of his implicit trust. I know things turned shitty, but he is a good guy. I think it might be a mistake to walk away."

"But what about my job?"

He shrugged. "I don't know what to say about that."

"I already made the sacrifice once, then he bulldozed me."

"I know."

I turned back to him.

"If he just didn't like your job, I would agree with him. But he is right...it's really dangerous. And he even said he would put up with it until you have kids. His head is in the right place if that's where he puts his foot down, over your kids. It shows he would be a good father. That's what a parent does—protects their kids."

"Yeah..."

Charlie turned silent and just stared at me.

But I didn't say anything.

"I know he's been a lot of work since you met, but I think he's worth it, Carson. You're so close to the finish line, you know?"

I ran my fingers through my hair and looked at the sandwich he'd brought for me. "I need to think about it."

"Don't take long. He seemed pretty angry the other night, and anger makes people do stupid things." He grabbed his sandwich then left my cubicle.

AT THE END of the workday, I took a cab across town and stepped into a busy bar where I would meet my source, who had agreed to talk on the condition of anonymity.

I was going to try to change his mind.

I found him sitting alone in the booth with a beer in front of him, glancing out the window over and over as if he were afraid he'd been followed.

I got my glass of wine from the bar then joined him.

He immediately stiffened when I sat down, letting out a deep breath like he'd been spooked by a ghost.

"We're perfectly safe. Relax."

He stared down at his hands, visibly distressed by this clandestine meeting. "Let's just get this over with."

I pulled out my recorder and set it on the table before I turned it on. I didn't take notes because I actually wanted to listen. "Tell me what you know."

He scanned the bar again to make sure no one was paying attention to us in the corner before he spoke. "I worked there for ten years. I was the chief lab scientist, and I was responsible for quality control and testing."

"How much fentanyl was cut into the drugs?"

"Triple the amount. Far exceeding the FDA guidelines."

"And there was no third-party scientist to verify your products for the FDA? They just take your word for it?"

"No, they do verify everything every quarter to make sure we're compliant."

I narrowed my eyes. "So, this goes up higher than just Kerosene?"

He nodded. "Why do you think I'm sweating like a pig right now?"

"Jesus... Can you give me names?"

"I can, but I shouldn't. My identity will be obvious."

I nodded. "But you do realize we can link Kerosene and the FDA in one of the biggest drug conspiracies in our nation's history? Jim, this is a really big deal. The government will write you a check, and you and your family can disappear—"

"I can't risk it. They'll get to me first. This is all the information I'm willing to tell you. You'll have to use this data and go digging yourself. That way, they know it wasn't me."

It was a lot to ask someone to risk their life, and judging from his disturbed countenance, I wouldn't get more than this out of him. I just had to be grateful. "Keep talking. I'm listening."

When I was finished with Jim, he left first.

I stayed to finish my glass of wine, to think about everything I'd learned about the biggest drug bust in history.

Now I understood why Simon Prescott had come on so strong.

I should be scared.

But all I could think about was Dax.

What was he doing at that moment? Was he home alone? Had he already moved on? If I came back to him, would he even want me?

I was used to independence and having full control over my life. And once I tried to share it with another person, I lost that control...and it terrified me. But that was how it had to be —no other way around it. Maybe I had to accept the chaos, the amount of work this relationship would take—because it was worth it.

I finished my wine before I left the bar and walked onto the sidewalk. There were a few people on the sidewalk but very limited cabs. But one drove by, and I waved it down.

Ever since my last encounter with Simon Prescott, I always made sure he wasn't lurking in the other seat before I got inside, so I bent down to check.

His shadowed outline was there.

I immediately turned away from the cab so I could sprint back into the bar.

Two guys came out of nowhere, one hand cupped over my mouth while the other got the door open. I was overpowered immediately, shoved into the car despite how hard I fought back. Then a fist flew at my face so hard that I saw stars.

My wrists and ankles were bound, and I was too dizzy to fight.

The door slammed shut, and the cab took off.

I turned to look at Simon, trying to fight the zip tie around my wrist. His face came in and out of focus.

He stared at me, shaking his head slightly. "What a shame…absolute shame." He grabbed my purse and found my phone. Then he slammed it down onto the center console, making the screen shatter. "Hope it was worth it, Carson."

27

DAX

I WENT BACK TO MY LONELY EXISTENCE.

It'd been a week, and she hadn't contacted me.

Her ring was still in my kitchen drawer, and now I knew she'd never come back to retrieve it.

My last attempt to get her back was cathartic, because I loved her deeply but had to speak my mind, that I wasn't the easiest person to deal with—but neither was she. I had my baggage, but I had a lot of qualities that would make me the perfect man to love her.

Letting me go was a mistake.

A big fucking mistake.

Letting her go was a mistake too, but I didn't let it happen. I fought until there was no other option.

I did the best I could.

I could continue to tell myself that until it didn't hurt anymore.

My phone rang, and Charlie's name appeared on the screen.

It was almost ten o'clock at night, so it was odd to hear from him. My heart started to race, wondering what he had to tell me. I took the call. "What's up?"

He spat out the words quickly. "Is Carson with you?"

"No... Why?"

"Oh shit."

The panic set in. "Why? Charlie, what's wrong?"

"She was supposed to talk to a source after work, but that was hours ago. She's not taking my texts or calls, and she *always* does. The girls tried to get a hold of her too, but nothing. When I call, it goes straight to voice mail, so I think her phone is off...or broken."

I was on my feet instantly, even though I had nowhere to go. "Did you call the police?"

"They won't file a missing person's report until she's been gone for twenty-four hours."

"Even though she's a reporter?" I asked incredulously.

"Yeah. I talked to the chief of police and everything. I know all the guys down there, but they still wouldn't do it."

Jesus, I was going to have a heart attack.

"I gotta go. I've got to make some calls—"

"What was her last location?"

"East of Eden in Brooklyn," Charlie said. "What are you going to do?"

"Find her."

"You're gonna go down there and ask questions? They're closed—"

"I'm going to hack in to her phone and pull up a location."

"You can do that?"

"You bet your fucking ass, I can." I hung up.

I MET my software guys at the office, called them in after hours and told them it was an emergency. They worked at their computers as they broke through the firewall of the operating system and actually got into the location services of her phone.

Charlie and Matt sat with the girls, helpless to do anything.

My lead engineer turned to me. "Sir, you know this is illegal—"

"I don't give a damn," I snapped. "They can lock me up afterward."

"Fair enough." He turned back in his chair and kept working.

"Any updates?" I asked, towering over them from behind.

"We're working as fast as we can," Tom said. "Just give some time."

I walked back to Carson's friends.

Charlie looked sick to his stomach. Denise cried on and off. Kat seemed like she was in shock. Matt was in a daze, like he had no idea what to do except stare at the wall.

I stood near them, my heart still racing like it was before.

"What do we do when we get her location?" Charlie asked.

"Call the cops and tell them there's a homicide in progress," I answered. "I just hope we get there in time." I continued to watch my guys work on their computers, breaking the privacy laws of this country and pulling a location from the software we created for the phones. In the past, the government had asked us to pull information from criminal's phones that could put them in jail for the rest of their lives, but we refused to cooperate because that violated our own code of ethics.

I didn't give a damn about ethics right now.

All I cared about was the woman I loved.

28

CARSON

When I opened my eyes, I was in a warehouse.

The windows were frosted from grime, not the cold. Big chains hung from the ceiling, like this place used to be a slaughterhouse. Everything was either metal or concrete. I couldn't recall how I got here, how I ended up in this chair, my legs and arms bound with duct tape.

They must have drugged me.

Once I was of sound mind, I started to twist to rip the tape. No use.

Voices sounded from behind me. "Boss, she's awake."

Simon Prescott's voice came a moment later. "Oh good. Let's get this show on the road."

I tried to fight again and again, but all I did was rock my chair until it tipped over, and I landed hard against the concrete.

"Careful." Simon Prescott grabbed my chair and tipped it back until I was upright once more. Then he moved in front of me, wearing his tailored suit. His hands slid into his pockets as he looked at me, a slight smile on his lips.

It was my time.

My nine lives had run out.

No amount of back talk would get me out of this one.

My body would be dumped into the bay, or I'd be stuffed in an oil drum. No one would find my body.

Dax would never know what happened to me.

The thought of him hurt the most.

One of Simon's cronies brought him a chair and set it down in front of me.

Simon took a seat without even glancing at it. He leaned back, put his hands together in his lap, and crossed his legs. "I warned you."

"Let me go, and I'll drop it." It was a demeaning thing to say because I would die for my career, but I thought about Dax and how heartbroken he would be that his worst nightmare had come true.

He cocked an eyebrow. "Really?"

"Yes."

"No. I mean, really, you're going to say that now?" He raised his hands and gestured to the warehouse where we sat, where the outside world was silenced. "Honey, there's no going back now. We both know that. But I can give you something else. Give me your sources, and I'll make it quick. A bullet to the back of the head. You won't even know when it's coming."

I heard one of his men step up behind me, like he had the gun pointed at the back of my head that very moment.

The panic dissipated when I knew there was no way out. I knew the risks when I took this job, made jokes about it like it wasn't a big deal. I had to accept my fate, and I had to do it with some dignity. That was how I wanted to spend my last few minutes on this earth. "You know I can't do that."

He pointed above him. "You see those chains?"

I didn't look.

"I'll hang you up by the ankle, and one of my boys will

torture you until you spit everything out. We've done it many times, and trust me, that's not how you want to go...with your fingernails ripped out, your eyelids carved off your face, until you're so disfigured that you don't even look like you anymore." His fingers interlocked on his lap as he stared at me, cocking his head slightly. "Tell me every source and every witness you've gathered. I'm going to figure it out anyway, it'll just take me longer."

"Liar." I was the key to the information. I left all my paperwork at the office so no one could break in to my apartment and steal it. If I kept the names a secret, they would live...and I was going to die anyway. "My fate is the same, regardless how it's delivered. So do what you have to do. Maybe others have talked, but I promise you, I won't. I never give up my sources. Not now. Not ever. And not for you."

Simon stared at me for a few seconds before he released a gentle breath. "What a shame. Such a pretty face." He lifted his gaze behind me and gave a slight nod to one of his men.

Here it comes.

Then sirens sounded in the distance.

Simon didn't react, assuming it was a police car zooming by to a crime scene. We were in a bad part of town where crime was rampant. But the sirens came closer and closer, until the red and blue lights lit up the window.

And there were at least a dozen cars—right outside the building.

It was the first time Simon Prescott didn't look like the cool and calculated suit that he was. He quickly turned to his men and nodded.

I knew he'd given the order to kill me.

I threw my body hard, so my chair toppled over.

The guy missed his shot and hit Simon Prescott in the leg.

He immediately collapsed, dirt covering his suit, blood dripping to his shoes. "What the fuck are you doing?"

It was pandemonium. Glass broke as the windows were shattered by bullets, and Simon continued to scream at his incompetent men. One of them ran to his side to lift him up from the floor and get him out of there, but then he was shot and collapsed to the floor.

I was on my side and strapped to the chair, seeing Simon grab his ankle then look at his palm, studying the blood smeared across his skin.

The police burst through the door, their guns aimed, covered in bulletproof vests.

Simon looked at me, furious.

I smiled.

The police swarmed into the warehouse and secured the perimeter. Some chased the cronies who had made it to the other side of the warehouse on foot. Others secured Simon Prescott in handcuffs instantly. And another came to me, lifting me from the chair and cutting the tape.

I guess I had more lives than I thought.

I DIDN'T HAVE a scratch on me other than my bruised eye, so I didn't have to be sent to the hospital. I was escorted out of the warehouse and to the sidewalk so I could be taken to the police station to give my statement.

A blanket was draped over my shoulders, and the officer escorted me to the car.

"Carson!" Charlie's loud voice came from behind me.

I quickly turned around and slammed the door shut so I could get to him.

He sprinted to me then gripped me tightly, squeezing me hard as he breathed in a rush. "Fuck, are you okay?" He pulled away and pulled off my blanket so he could look at me. His hands touched me everywhere, checking for bullet wounds, even though I was fine.

"Charlie, I'm okay." I placed my hands on his chest. "It was Simon Prescott. But I don't think we need to worry about him anymore."

"Jesus..."

"How did you even know I was here?"

His eyes softened. "When I knew you were missing—"

"Sis!" Denise ran into me next and nearly knocked me over. "Oh my god..."

Kat and Matt came after her, rushing into me and holding me, surrounding me in a group hug that was more bulletproof.

I closed my eyes and cherished the love. I was reunited with my friends, reunited with my family. My life had almost been taken from me, but I was given another chance...for some reason. "I'm okay, you guys. How did you know I was here?"

They dispersed sideways so there was an open path in front of me.

And that was when I saw Dax, his eyes wet with tears, his breathing hard like he was about to collapse right on the pavement. The longer he stared at me, the wetter his eyes became, unashamed of the emotion that took him.

Charlie spoke from beside me. "He was the one who found you and told the police. He traced your phone."

Dax came closer to me, his eyes shifting back and forth like he couldn't believe I was real, that I was standing in front of him.

I hadn't thought about how the police knew where I was. It all happened so quickly, and I didn't think twice about it. But now, it didn't make sense. No one would have figured out where I'd gone in time to save me. "You saved my life..."

He moved farther into me until his hands slid to my cheeks, bringing our bodies close together, the tears in his eyes growing so large that they dripped down his cheeks. All he did was give a nod because he didn't have the ability to speak.

My friends started to back away so we could have some space.

Charlie said one final thing before he stepped back. "He broke a lot of laws to find you, used his engineers to hack into the OS system on your phone, then called the police." He moved away with the gang.

I never took my eyes off Dax.

He pressed his forehead to mine and held me close, inhaling a deep breath when we were reunited. "Are you okay?"

"Yeah..."

The officer gave us some time, but then he opened the back door again. "Ma'am, we need you to give that statement down at the precinct."

I didn't want to leave, but I knew I had to finish this.

Dax pulled his hands away, even though it seemed to take all his strength to do it.

There was so much I wanted to say, but I didn't know how to say it. So, I just said the first thing that came to mind. "I'm sorry..."

His hands moved to mine, and he gripped them.

"Take me back..." I'd thought I would never see his face again, see the man I loved with my whole heart. Once he was gone, I'd realized what I had lost, that I was just as complicated as he was.

He slid one hand into his pocket, grabbed something, and then placed it in my palm before he closed my fingers around it.

I could feel it. This time, I knew it wasn't a key.

It was my ring.

I opened my fingers, looked at it, and started to cry.

He watched me, his eyes still wet.

I slid it back onto my left hand, where it should have stayed in the first place.

"I'll wait for you at the apartment. When you get back, we'll go home."

I smiled through my tears.

He cupped my face again and kissed me. "I love you."

I grabbed on to him and didn't know how I would ever let go, how I would ever part with the man who completed my soul. "I love you."

29

CARSON

I stepped into Vince's office and set the article on his desk along with the digital copy. "It's done."

He didn't grab it right away like he usually did. He didn't grab that ugly red pen to mark it up and rip it apart. He just stared at me. "I'm sure it's great, Carson."

I gave a slight smile.

"You doing okay?"

"Yeah." I touched the area around my bruised eye, which had improved significantly over the last few days. "It feels a lot better than it looks. And honestly, it could have been so much worse, so...no complaints."

He nodded. "I'm happy you're doing well. Not sure what I would have done if we'd lost you."

"Well...I have some bad news on that front—"

"I meant you as a person, Carson. Not a reporter."

My eyes began to water slightly.

"I assumed you would be stepping down. You've accomplished more than reporters twice your age. I think it's okay for you to retire, let someone else carry the torch. And good news, I've got an opening in the Lifestyle section." He grinned.

I rolled my eyes. "God, I'd rather be a hot dog vendor on the street."

He chuckled. "You wouldn't last. You'd eat everything and have nothing to sell."

"Yeah. Probably."

"So, you want your old job back?" he asked. "The prime minister is no Simon Prescott, but he's got his merits."

"Yes, I'll take it. I'm excited to slow down."

He grabbed my article and set it to the side like he intended to read it when I left his office. "How's your boyfriend doing?"

"Fiancé," I corrected, holding up my ring. "And he's just happy that I'm okay."

He straightened in his chair and grabbed the paper. "You haven't heard the news, I take it?"

My eyes narrowed.

He held up the front-page headline. "The Feds hit him with a hundred million dollar fine for breaching the privacy laws. He'll have that on his record forever."

"Shit..." I had no idea.

He shrugged. "If he hadn't done it, you'd be dead. So I have a feeling he doesn't regret it."

30

DAX

I stood at my desk and read the notice several times, even though I'd already absorbed all the information I needed to know. My lawyer said there was no way to dispute it, and it was smart just to pay it and make it go away.

Renee stood with her arms crossed over her chest. "How do you think this will affect the company?"

I shrugged. "Scandals come and go. People will forget in the next news cycle."

"But people will never trust our software again, not when we pulled a stunt like that."

"I did what I had to do to save Carson—and I don't regret it." She was beside me every night again, but it was still hard for me to sleep. The terror of the situation had traumatized me, because I had to confront the possibility that she could have died...and I would have died. It made me realize how much I loved her, how deep that love really went.

"I don't either. But I think we need to work on damage control, regaining the public's trust—"

Carson stepped inside my office but stilled when she realized Renee was there. "I'll just wait outside—"

"Sweetheart, come here." She could walk into my office whenever the hell she wanted.

She hesitated before she came inside and approached us. She looked uncertain, like she'd just heard the news. "I'm sorry about—"

Renee hugged her tightly. "I'm so glad you're alright. What a fucking nightmare." She rubbed Carson's back before she pulled away.

Carson looked visibly surprised, like she didn't expect affection. "Thank you." She turned to me next. "Vince told me the news when I submitted my article. I'm sorry that this has happened to you."

My arm moved around her waist, and I pulled her in for a kiss. "I couldn't care less, Carson."

She melted right before my eyes, like my sister wasn't standing there. "I stepped down. I'll be back to my other position."

We hadn't even had a conversation about it. I knew she would do it on her own.

"And my last article will be my legacy—and it'll be a good one."

I kissed her forehead and pulled away.

She crossed her arms over her chest. "Is everything okay here? That's a lot of money."

Renee shrugged. "Not really. That's not what we're most concerned about."

Carson turned to me. "What are you most concerned about?"

"Sales," I answered. "Trust from our customers. Our brand going forward."

"But you did it to save my life," she whispered. "That doesn't make any sense."

I shrugged. "That's not what people hear. They just see the headline that I broke the law."

She dropped her chin and considered what I said, her eye

still slightly discolored but almost back to normal. "I have an idea." She lifted her chin again. "I'll write another editorial about you, about how you did everything you could to save my life...because we're in love."

"Would your editor let you run an article like that?" Renee asked in surprise.

"Oh, my editor will let me print whatever the hell I want," Carson said. "It's not something we usually do, but I think it'll bring the spotlight on to your heroic actions rather than your criminal activity, and you'll be more popular than you were before."

"I think that sounds like a great idea." Renee turned to me. "What do you think?"

My eyes were on Carson, a soft smile on my lips. "I love it."

Carson's belongings had been returned to the penthouse. Her makeup was on my bathroom counter, her panties on my bedroom floor because she never put them in the hamper, not that I minded in the least, and there was always a cord across the bedroom floor because she constantly needed to charge her laptop since she used it every second of the day.

Life was good.

Simon Prescott wasn't granted bail, so he wasn't going anywhere.

Carson's article was revolutionary, exposing the conspiracy between the biggest pharmaceutical company and a government agency that was supposed to keep us all safe from horrible shit like that.

It was a great way for her to move on.

Like when Peyton Manning won his last Super Bowl then retired.

I was proud of her beyond belief—but also grateful that it was over.

I would never have to worry about her again.

Our lives could be simple now, just two people in love who went to work every day and came home to each other, with game nights on the weekends, basketball on Wednesdays, absorbing her friends as my own.

I was happy.

The elevator doors opened, and I stepped inside the penthouse.

Carson immediately jumped off the couch and moved into my arms. "Hey." Her arms wrapped around my neck, and she kissed me, kissed me like we'd been apart for eight weeks instead of eight hours. "Guess what?"

"What?" I smiled as I looked down at her, the woman who was my whole world.

"My article came out today." She moved away and grabbed the paper sitting on the couch.

"About the prime minister?"

"No. No one cares about that." She held up the paper, and on the front page was the headline. *How Clydesdale Software Saved My Life*.

I took the paper from her hand and started to read.

"*As a reporter for the New York Press, my life has been on the line more times than I can count. But as a cat with nine lives, I've always managed to slip away.*

But not this time.

Simon Prescott continued to threaten my life if I didn't cease my investigation into his criminal activity, poisoning millions of Americans and purposely making them sick just to increase Kerosene Pharmaceuticals' profits. Even the FDA was on their payroll. But this information was too important not to be exposed, so I continued my investigation.

Until he grabbed me and threw me into a cab. Moments later, I was in a warehouse. And if I didn't give up my sources, they would rip my eyelids off my face, carve my lips off my mouth, but I never give up my sources, so I accepted the torture.

But out of nowhere, the police arrived...and saved my life.

The only reason they knew my location was because of my fiancé.

You know him as Dax Frawley, CEO of Clydesdale Software.

He knew the police would never find me in time, so he did something he knew was illegal before he did it. He violated all the privacy laws of this country and hacked in to the operating system of my phone to obtain my location from software his company designed, even though my phone was smashed beyond recognition. He used every tool at his disposal—to save the woman he loves.

He's been hit a hundred million dollar fine, leaving a black mark that will be forever on his record.

His response? "I would do it again in a heartbeat."

Because he would do anything for the woman he loves.

Me.

The article continued, but I lifted my gaze and looked at her again. "You make me look pretty good."

"I made you look like a hero, which is what you are."

I tossed the newspaper back onto the table and wrapped my arms around her. I cherished the gift of this moment, being able to hold her, to look into her beautiful face. If things hadn't unfolded the way they did, she would have disappeared...and I never would have found her.

My life would be a bitter and sad story.

But she was here with me.

Right this very moment.

"What are you doing tomorrow?" She lowered her voice, like she could see the thoughts printed across my eyes.

"Nothing. Why?"

"You want to get married?"

"On a Wednesday?" I asked in surprise.

"Yeah. Just as soon as possible."

I cupped her cheek and saw the love in her eyes, the eagerness to be with me forever. "I think that's a great idea."

"I asked for a couple weeks off at work. Thought we could go somewhere, have a honeymoon."

"I think that's an even better idea." I pulled her close and rested my forehead against hers, inhaling a deep breath because I felt at peace, truly at peace. My past was long forgotten, and I was finally where I was meant to be. "Where do you want to go?"

"I don't care. Somewhere that has a bed and drinks."

"What about food?"

"Oh yeah. That too."

"Have you been to the Caribbean?"

"Ugh, I've never been on vacation."

"Then you're going to love it. I'll make the arrangements."

"You can take time off work like that?"

My hand squeezed her ass. "Trust me, Renee will be happy to get rid of me."

31

CARSON

I walked into the apartment with my bag over my shoulder. "I'm baaaaaack!"

Charlie stood in the kitchen in just his boxers, while Denise wore his t-shirt, her hair messy.

Charlie quickly grabbed the dish towel and wrapped it around his waist. "What are you doing here?"

"Oh, calm down," I said. "I've already seen your hot dog. Not interested." I set my bag on the table then draped my wedding dress in the garment bag over the back of the couch. "So, Dax and I decided to get married tomorrow. We thought we should sleep apart one last time."

"Oh my god, you're getting married?" Denise came over to me and gave me a big hug. "Aw, I'm so happy for you."

"And then we're going to the Caribbean for a fuck-a-thon," I said.

"Even better." Denise pulled away and smiled at me.

Charlie grabbed the blanket off the back of the couch and tied it around his body like a toga. "Congratulations, Carson. Happy for you." He gave me a hug and then a kiss on my hairline, something he never did. He was a lot more affectionate with me after I almost died. It seemed to affect him as much as it affected Dax.

"So, it's cool if I crash here?" I asked. "We can do a little bachelorette party. Get some pizzas and beers and dance on the couch?"

"I think that sounds like a great idea," Denise said. "I'll call Matt and Kat. I'll tell them to come over in an hour, give us some time to look presentable."

"You guys look as happy as Dax and me," I said, my eyes shifting back and forth between them. "It's nice."

Charlie wrapped his arm around her shoulders and gave her a kiss on the side of the head. "We are. Life has been good to us."

My eyes softened before I turned back to the couch. "You want to see my dress?"

"Please." Denise stood close to Charlie's side, not self-conscious that she was just in his shirt and nothing else.

I unzipped the bag and displayed it.

"Wow," Charlie said. "That's nice."

"Oh my god, it's gorgeous." My sister's eyes started to water before she looked at me. "You're going to be the most beautiful bride ever."

"And the most scandalous," I said. "Look at that slit."

"And that boobage in the front," Charlie said. "It's totally you."

"I wonder if you'll even be able to get married wearing that," Denise said. "Dax will be too distracted to say 'I do.'"

"I got some slutty lingerie to wear underneath, too," I said. "That way, after he takes it off me, he'll have something else to look forward to." I zipped the dress back up and returned it to the couch. "So, let's party tonight, but not too much. A hungover bride never looks good."

32

DAX

"You look awfully sharp for a courthouse," Jeremy said, coming to me and patting me on the shoulder.

"Wait until you see my bride." I knew what her dress looked like, and I knew she'd look like a damn bombshell in it. And whatever was underneath was even more beautiful. I adjusted my cuff links.

Clint came to me, his hands in his pockets. "So, no more strip clubs?"

I shook my head.

"No more parties in the clubs downtown?"

I shook my head again. "Sorry, man."

He shrugged. "If you're happy, that's all that matters...I guess."

It was the first time I had my two groups of friends together, and they got along well. We stood together inside the courthouse, all of us about to pile into a small room so we could have the quick ceremony. It wasn't grand like my last wedding, but it was much better.

Because I got the bride right this time.

The last group of people left, and we said congratulations to the bride and groom before we filed inside. There were a few chairs, and the officiant was there. Renee and William walked in, holding hands.

"You afraid she's going to stand you up?" Jeremy asked.

"She might," Nathan said. "She's a lot hotter than you."

"No, she'll be here," I said. "Just wants to look perfect."

A few minutes later, Carson stepped inside in her wedding dress, her friends around her all dressed up for the occasion. The white dress was tight around her petite waist, and the high slit allowed her gorgeous leg to emerge, all toned and tanned, sexy in her white heels. Her tits were pushed together in the low-cut front, and her hair was in sexy curls.

Jesus Christ...that's my wife.

Jeremy gave a nod of approval. "Damn."

Carson smiled when she looked at me, like I was the only person in the room whom she noticed. Her friends walked with her then stayed back so it could just be the two of us in front of the officiant. She came to me and immediately wrapped her arms around my neck to kiss me, to disregard the customs of a wedding and just do whatever she wanted.

I loved that about her.

I held her close as I kissed her, my arms squeezing her small frame against me. "You look beautiful, sweetheart."

"You do too."

I kissed her again, forgetting that other people were there.

Charlie cleared his throat. "Are we going to see a wedding or...?"

"Free porn?" Clint teased.

I smiled slightly before I released her and stepped back.

The officiant cleared his throat like he was uncomfortable with the make-out session we'd just had. "Alright, let's get started." With his bible tucked under his arm and his courthouse form in hand, he started the ceremony.

I barely listened, too engrossed in her beauty to pay attention to what he said. Her eyes were brighter than they'd ever been, and her lips were in a smile more genuine than I'd ever seen before. When she spoke, I was pulled back to what we were doing.

"I do." She squeezed my hands.

The officiant turned to me. "Do you take this woman to be your lawfully wedded wife—"

"Fuck yes."

Everyone laughed at my response.

Carson chuckled. "Oh, I'll never forget that. I'll tell our kids someday."

The officiant continued. "I now pronounce you—"

Carson jumped into my arms and wrapped her legs around my waist, the slit in her dress opening to reveal her entire leg. Her lips moved to mine, and she kissed me hard.

It was the sexiest thing she'd ever done.

Everyone clapped and cheered.

The officiant continued. "Husband and wife. You may kiss the bride."

My hands gripped her ass as I held her, kissing her like no one was in the room; it was only us two. Our lives had just begun, but I was eager to live through it all, to have babies with her, to grow old with her, to look back on our lives and know we lived it to the fullest—with each other.

I SAT on the edge of the bed, stripped down to my boxers, looking at my bride as she stood in front of me. We were in our penthouse, and we had all night before we left on our honeymoon tomorrow afternoon. But it didn't feel like the penthouse I'd lived in for almost a decade. It felt like a special place because everything was different now.

Carson was my wife.

She stood before me and slowly unzipped the back of her dress, taking her time as she stripped in front of me, letting the white material slowly come loose from her body and slide down her body, revealing the see-through white teddy underneath, the crotchless bottom that would allow me to have her without even taking it off.

I liked it just as much as her dress.

She stepped out of her dress then walked to me in her sky-high heels, leaving them on so she could strut to me like a goddamn fantasy.

Fuck...I wasn't going to last long.

She straddled my hips and sat on my lap, my arms securing her to me so she wouldn't fall back. Her arms circled my neck, and she looked into my face for a moment, seeing my reaction to her, feeling my hardness through my boxers.

She leaned in and kissed me on the mouth slowly, so slow that it was agonizing, and then she gradually picked up speed, her hands exploring my chest and shoulders, her wet pussy soaking the front of my boxers.

She placed her palms against my shoulders and gently pushed me back, bringing me flat on the bed. She tugged my boxers down then leaned over me, prepared to arch her back and ride me, consummate this marriage in the sexiest way possible.

My hands dug into her hair and pulled it from her face so I could look at her as she slid down my length until I was entirely buried within her. Her lips parted as she released a quiet moan, like it was our first time, like every sensation was brand-new.

My hands gripped her ass, and I released a loud moan, like a caveman who couldn't control his response.

When she was finally full of me, her palms flattened against my chest, and she started to rock into me, ride my length to my base then slowly come up again. She made love to me as her husband, taking me with a gentleness that was so sexy it made my body go weak.

My feet pressed against the frame of the bed, and I lifted

my hips to slide inside her, to match her pace, to savor every sensation between our wet bodies. "Sweetheart..."

She leaned forward so she could bring her face close to mine. "It's Mrs. Frawley..."

Another groan escaped my lips, a loud explosion, a tremble that overtook my entire body. I never asked her to change her last name because I assumed she would refuse. Guess I was wrong. And the fact that she did...was the sexiest thing ever. "Goddamn, Mrs. Frawley."

EPILOGUE
DAX

I pulled up to the curb and parked.

Kent and Melanie sat on the bench together, both wearing their backpacks as they waited for me to pick them up. They didn't notice me because they were both looking down at the ground at a bug.

I honked my horn.

They both looked up then walked to the car.

Kent got into the passenger seat beside me, and Melanie got into the back.

"Hey, Dad," Kent said.

I moved my fingers into his hair for a quick rub before I pulled onto the road. "Hey, son. How was school?"

"Boring." He looked out the window. He was ten years old, getting to the age when he was less excited about things than he used to be.

I looked in the rearview mirror at Melanie in the back. "What about you, honey?"

"I fed a squirrel some nuts at recess." She kicked her feet back and forth as she looked out the window, still wearing her pink backpack. She was a few years younger than her brother. She had Carson's green eyes and also her feistiness.

"Are you supposed to be doing that?" I asked as I kept my eyes on the road.

"Probably not," Melanie said. "But I don't care."

I smiled slightly as I kept driving. "Doesn't surprise me."

I drove to the penthouse and parked in the underground garage before we rode the elevator to our floor. When we walked in, I got them both seated at the dining table so they could work on their homework. I made them a snack then got to work on making dinner.

Carson texted me. *I'm going to be late tonight. The guy I'm interviewing is late...asshole.*

It's fine. Don't worry about it.

How are the kids?

Doing their homework. I'm making dinner.

What's on the menu?

Tacos.

Goddammit...this motherfucker better hurry the hell up.

LOL. They'll be here when you get back.

Kent spoke from the dining table. "Dad, I don't know what the teacher wants me to do..."

I put the phone down. "I'll be right there, son." Carson had different hours than I did, so she didn't pick up the kids from school often. I had reduced my hours at the office, but Renee and I decided to share the CEO position since we both had kids now and just didn't have the time to be in charge fully. Carson made up for her absence by taking care of the kids all day on the weekends.

It allowed me to sleep in—which was a godsend.

THE FOUR OF us sat together at the dining table, eating our tacos and talking about our day.

"Your dad tells me you fed a squirrel today?" Carson asked as she poured more hot sauce on her tacos.

"Yep," Melanie said. "I see him every day at recess and give him my food."

"You give him food every day?" Carson asked incredulously. "Baby, I make that food for you, not a squirrel."

"But you're always telling me to share..." Melanie dropped her gaze and pushed her dinner around.

Carson's eyes softened as she looked at our daughter. "True...but I meant with other kids, not animals. But that's very sweet, Melanie." She turned to Kent. "How was your day?"

"I suck at math," Kent spat out. "Dad's been helping me, but..."

"I'll help you tomorrow, alright?"

When we finished dinner, Carson did the dishes and then sat with them on the couch, watching TV and spending time with them so I could have some alone time in our room, going over emails and paperwork with the game on in the background.

After she put them to bed, she walked into the bedroom and stepped into my closet. "Now, it's my favorite part of the day."

"Yeah?" I grinned as I shut my laptop and set it on my nightstand.

She stepped out of the walk-in closet in a black teddy and garters.

I looked her up and down and gave a quiet whistle.

"I'm gonna give my husband a nice blow job for being such a good father."

I interlocked my fingers behind my head and gave a shrug. "I'm a good father because I want to be, but I'm not gonna say no to that." I nodded toward my lap. "Come on down, sweetheart. Show me what you got."

She got onto the bed and started to crawl toward me. "Oh, I will..."

Printed in Great Britain
by Amazon